BURYING THE SUN

BURYING THE SUN

ALSO BY GLORIA WHELAN

CHU JU'S HOUSE

THE IMPOSSIBLE JOURNEY

FRUITLANDS

ANGEL ON THE SQUARE

HOMELESS BIRD

MIRANDA'S LAST STAND

INDIAN SCHOOL

The Island Trilogy:

ONCE ON THIS ISLAND

FAREWELL TO THE ISLAND

RETURN TO THE ISLAND

GLORIA WHELAN

BURYING THE SUN

HARPERCOLLINS*PUBLISHERS*

Library of Congress Cataloging-in-Publication Data
Whelan, Gloria.
  Burying the sun / Gloria Whelan.— 1st ed.
    p.   cm.
  Includes bibliographical references (p.).
  Summary: In Leningrad in 1941, when Russia and
Germany are at war, fourteen-year-old Georgi vows to help
his family and his city during the terrible siege.
  ISBN 0-06-054112-1 — ISBN 0-06-054113-X (lib. bdg.)
  1. Saint Petersburg (Russia)—History—Siege,
1941–1944—Juvenile fiction. [1. Saint Petersburg
(Russia)—History—Siege, 1941–1944—Fiction. 2. Soviet
Union—History—German occupation, 1941–1944—
Fiction. 3. World War, 1939–1945—Russia (Federation)—
Saint Petersburg—Fiction. 4. Famines—Fiction.
5. Survival—Fiction.] I. Title.
PZ7.W5718Dar 2004
[Fic]—dc22   2003012487
                                                         CIP
                                                          AC

1 3 5 7 9 10 8 6 4 2
❖
First Edition

To Susan Rich

In Petersburg we'll meet again,
As though we'd buried the sun there.

—from *Tristia* by Osip Mandelstam,
translated by Bruce A. McClelland

BURYING THE SUN

CHAPTER ONE

THE SUMMER GARDEN

June 21, 1941

Later that day everything would change, but on that afternoon the six of us were sprawled on the lawn of Leningrad's Summer Garden, our stomachs full, our picnic baskets empty. The last of the ice had long since drifted down the Neva, and now sailboats were sweeping along the river "like the wings of giant seagulls." That was how Yelena described them. Like me, Yelena was nearly fifteen. She was a poet and looked the way you would imagine a poet looked, with lilacs tucked into her long honey-colored braid and a flowered dress. She was small, while I was a skinny six feet, so I always felt like a giant next to her. Though she looked delicate, she was as quick as a rabbit. When we raced each other, she could run as fast as I could.

"Georgi," she would taunt me, "catch me if you can." Off she would go, laughing at me as I raced to keep up. School was over, and Yelena was going to work in the Leningrad Public Library among the books she loved. "Rooms full of them, Georgi," she said, "maybe a million, and I'm going to read every one."

I would be working among the thousands of paintings at the Hermitage, the great museum that was a part of the Winter Palace. While Yelena was checking out books, I would be pushing a mop. What I really wanted to do was repair cars, which is something I'm good at. There aren't many automobiles in Leningrad, so the auto mechanic who lets me fool around in his shop couldn't afford to pay me to work for him. My sister, Marya, found me the job at the Hermitage. She works as a secretary to the director.

That afternoon in the Summer Garden, my mother

was there along with Marya. Yelena had come with her mother, Olga, and her grandfather Viktor. Yelena's family, the Daskals, like our family, had been arrested for opposing Stalin and exiled to Siberia. Yelena's father, like my father, had died there. Five years ago we had returned to Leningrad—St. Petersburg, Mama still called the city.

We all had new lives now. We had put the misery of Siberia behind us. Viktor was a bookkeeper at an aircraft factory, and Olga played the violin in the Leningrad Radio Symphony. Mama worked as a nurse at the Erisman Hospital.

Yelena's grandfather Viktor still lived in the past. I think he was bitter because he had survived and his son had not. He had a long face, pinched in at the cheeks with great pouches under his watery eyes. The corners of his mouth were ever turned downward. Even Yelena, who could cheer anyone up, could not make him smile.

"Katya Ivanova," Viktor said to Mama, "I am

ashamed to be a Russian. It sickens me that we should be allies with those Nazi barbarians."

Nearly two years before, in 1939, Russia and Germany had signed a friendship treaty. Russia closed its eyes while Germany fought England and the rest of Europe. Russia had even shared in the spoils as Germany stole one country after another, marching into Poland and Finland and the Baltic countries, swallowing them up like a greedy child.

"Russia has left behind a trail of death and suffering, Viktor Alexandrovich," Mama said. "I have a terrible feeling we will pay for our sins." Even though there was no one near us, all this was said in a quiet voice, for any words against the government were dangerous.

"Grandfather," Yelena pleaded, tickling him with a dandelion, "must you spoil our picnic with your gloomy thoughts?"

My sister agreed. "There is nothing we can do about such things now, so why make ourselves miserable?"

And then she added, "But the day of reckoning will come for us. Germany will turn against us. You can't trust her. Andrei told me German soldiers and tanks are threatening our borders. He says the General Staff is waiting for orders from Stalin to get ready to fight the Germans, but the orders never come. Stalin only says rumors of Germany breaking the treaty and attacking us are a plot by the British to get us to fight on their side against Germany." Andrei was an officer in the Red Army assigned to the General Staff Building. He and Marya were engaged, and for Marya, Andrei's word was law.

In spite of all the pessimistic things that were being said, it was a perfect summer day, and I tried to put such worries aside. Yet I could not forget what had happened with the *Lützow*. The *Lützow* was a great cruiser that Russia had bought from Germany. It had been towed to the Leningrad shipyards. My friend Dmitry Trushin and I often walked over after school to watch the German shipbuilders readying the

Lützow for duty. The Germans were hard workers and friendly. I had hoped they might take me on as a helper. We came so often, they recognized us and would look up from their work and wave to us. Then their number began to grow smaller. Not one German shipbuilder remained, and yet there was still a lot of work to be done on the cruiser. Dmitry and I couldn't figure it out. Why had the shipbuilders gone back to Germany?

Marya's talk of a war with Germany may have answered the question, but on so fine a day I didn't want to think about such things. I swallowed the last of the *krendeli*, the little heart-shaped cookies that Olga had baked, and took Yelena's hand. Together we wandered away from the frightening talk. I chased Yelena around the fountain and in and out among the trees and statues until I caught her and, looking quickly to see that no one was near, kissed her.

She darted away, calling over her shoulder, "I dare you to try that again."

University students recovering from their graduation parties of the night before were resting on the ground, as lifeless as fallen trees. Children had taken off their shoes and socks and were splashing about in the fountain. One boy, braver than the others, climbed right into the fountain's spout and stood there, mouth open and eyes closed, as the waters washed over him. I could tell Yelena was tempted to jump in herself.

Yelena and I settled down on a bench. The next day there was to be a soccer game at the Dynamo Stadium. I emptied my pockets, carefully counting my money to be sure I had enough for one of the cheap seats. Yelena shook her head.

"For the same money," she said, "you could get a ticket for the ballet. Ulanova is dancing *Romeo and Juliet*."

It was our old argument. She wanted me to read poetry and go to the ballet. Yelena lived in her own world, where only good and beautiful things existed. If there was ugliness, she would not admit it. She could even turn war into something beautiful. Secretly she wrote poems about the noble Finns and Poles who fought for their independence against Russia. She had showed one of the poems to me.

The Russian eagle's cruel beak
seeks a prey small and weak.
Blood on Finland's white snow—
we shut our eyes, still we know.

I had watched as she tore the poem into little pieces, little bits of herself gone forever. You didn't dare to criticize the government. Yelena remembered Siberia as well as I did.

It was early evening before Yelena and I followed the others down Leningrad's main boulevard, the Nevsky Prospekt. It was June 21, the summer solstice, the longest day of the year. Everyone was in a mood to celebrate. The summer of white nights was here. There would be no darkness tonight, only a thin veil across the sun in the early-morning hours. The crowded cafés and stores would be open all night. At one of the flower stalls I bought Yelena a single yellow daffodil. She laughed at me.

"You are a romantic after all, Georgi."

I said good-bye to Yelena at her door and went into our own apartment next door. The wall between our apartments was like an eggshell, and I could soon hear Olga practicing some lively piece on her violin. I sometimes wondered if she didn't take up her violin to drown out the sound of Viktor's grumbling.

If Viktor was too pessimistic, Olga was just the opposite. Like Yelena, she saw everything in a sunny light. If there was a shortage of white flour, she said there was nothing so good as a buckwheat *blini*. If the Daskals' apartment was tiny, she said they were living as cozily as kittens in a basket. Olga was a romantic, dressing like a Gypsy with long skirts and fringed shawls. We all loved her for her cheerfulness.

In our apartment Marya had her head buried in one of her art books and Mama was laying out clothes for her work at the hospital the next day, which was Sunday. Before the revolution Sunday had been a day for church and rest, but now it was a workday like any other. Few churches were open. The great St. Isaac's Cathedral, where Mama had worshiped with the tsar and his family, was now the Museum of Atheism.

I went out onto the balcony. It was the best thing about our apartment, which was only a mousehole with a cupboard of a bedroom for Marya and Mama and a sitting room with a bit of kitchen and a couch where I slept. The balcony, a great luxury, was left over from the time when our building of small apartments had been a mansion. In the winter the balcony was covered with snow, but in the summer it was like a front porch.

I settled down on the bench we kept there and spent the next hour gazing at the people who were walking up and down the prospekt enjoying the white night. A friend from school called up to me, and I returned his greeting. It was a great relief to have the semester over. I had one more year of school, and then I meant to apply to the Academy of Sciences. I hoped to study geography. One day I would go back to Siberia, not as an exile but as a famous scientist.

It was after midnight and the sun was still shining when Mama told me to get ready for bed. "Tomorrow is your first day at the museum, and you had better be rested." She smiled. "The brooms and mops won't do their work by themselves, Georgi." I was glad enough to have the job so that I could help Mama out, but I hated the thought of spending all my summer days shut up in a stuffy museum.

Since there was no darkness, when I was awakened by a pounding on the door, I had no idea of the time. I looked at the clock and saw that it was only five in the morning. A loud knocking on the door was a sign to everyone of danger. I had never forgotten the night the police had pounded on our door and taken

Mama and Papa away.

Marya and Mama hurried from their small bedroom into the living room. They had hastily thrown on their robes. Mama gave us a warning glance and opened the door a crack. With relief we saw it was only Marya's fiancé, Andrei, but there was nothing in his behavior to take away our worry. Even now, in his excitement, he was in perfect order, tall and straight, his sandy hair cut short, his cap just so, his boots like two mirrors. I envied him his uniform, but I knew it was dangerous to be an officer in the Red Army. In Stalin's terrible purges half of the officers of the army had been executed, which was why Andrei, who was only twenty-three, was already a lieutenant.

"I have just come from a meeting at the General Staff Building," Andrei said. "Lieutenant General Popov has sent me on an errand to Party headquarters, and this was just a block off my path. I have only a second, but I wanted to warn you. The Germans have detained our ships, and they are moving their tanks closer to our borders. German planes have been overflying Russia. A defector from the German army says the Germans mean to attack us this very day. It will surely mean war. God help Leningrad; we are not prepared."

His arm was around Marya, and I was startled to see tears in his eyes. It had never occurred to me that a soldier might cry. The tears alarmed me more than anything he said.

He was already at the door. "I came to tell you to get some food," he said, "as much as you can afford. Soon we will all be starving." He gave Marya a last long look and shook hands with me, man to man, which he had never done before. A moment later he was gone.

The early-morning sun was bright, but Andrei's frightening warning was like an invisible black cloud filling the apartment. I was sure our lives would change, but I couldn't guess how. It seemed to me that by his handshake Andrei was letting me know that

I now had some responsibility, but what could a fourteen-year-old boy do?

"I won't take more than our share," Mama was saying, "but we are low on sugar and flour. I must get to the stores before I go to the hospital."

Mama got ready at once, not even stopping for breakfast. As if she could read my mind, she turned to me as she was going out the door and said, "Georgi, don't do anything foolish."

Marya and I had a hurried breakfast of bread and jam. Marya poured tea for the two of us. We sat together at the small wooden table. Though we were five years apart, and though she was always trying to organize me, as if I were a drawer and my actions so many socks and shirts that would stay where you put them, we were close.

When I was eight and Marya was thirteen, we traveled together a thousand miles across Siberia to find our mother. We knew we could never have survived without each other, but I had become so used to her, I took her for granted. She was always just there. Now, for the first time in many months, I studied my sister and was surprised to see how grown-up she looked, with her hair pulled back into a fancy knot and her face carefully made up. Although I would never tell her so, I decided she was very pretty.

She asked, "Georgi, how can we fight the Germans? Their army is huge. They have tanks and bombers, and Andrei says we are unprepared."

"Yes, but Germany's army is scattered all over Europe. They send their bombers over England. They have to have soldiers in France to keep order, and the Netherlands and Belgium and Poland, and there is talk of their taking Greece. With all of that going on, I can't figure out why they are turning on us."

"Andrei says they want our wheat and our oil, that they can never defeat England without them."

"If Germany fights us," I said, trying to figure things out, "we will be on the side of England." For years Stalin had been telling us that England and

America were our enemies.

Marya took my hand in hers. "Georgi, if there is war, what will happen to Andrei? He might be sent to the front and killed."

I tried to cheer her. "No, you'll see. They will keep him right here on the General Staff to run the war. He is too efficient to send away."

"Don't make jokes, Georgi. I'm frightened." Even when Marya had marched into the office of the secret police to find out where our parents were, she had not admitted to being afraid.

She stood up, anxious as always for some action. "I have to hurry to the Hermitage, but there's no point in your starting work today, Georgi. Everything will be confusion until we find out what is fact and what is rumor. If there is truly going to be a war, you will live at the Hermitage for many weeks, and so will I."

"What do you mean?"

"The museum is full of masterpieces. We can't leave them to be destroyed or stolen by the Germans."

Stolen by the Germans. That meant Marya was thinking that the Germans would march into Leningrad. I said nothing, but I resolved that I would not spend the war in a museum. As soon as Marya was gone, I hurried to the bedroom and looked into the mirror. Staring back at me was a face with even features, blue eyes that tilted down a bit at the corners, brown hair that looked chopped rather than cut, and a ruddy complexion still with a sprinkling of adolescent pimples. If I was honest, I would have to admit I looked little more than my age. I tried to think what I could do to pass for eighteen, the age at which you could enlist in the army.

CHAPTER TWO

ШДR

June 22, 1941

I didn't want to stay in the apartment when everything was happening somewhere else. I wanted to talk things over with my friend Dmitry, but he would be at his job washing dishes at the Hotel Europa.

I wandered over to Fontanska Street and the offices of the newspaper, *Leningradskaya Pravda*, where news bulletins were often pinned to a board. There was nothing about a war with the Germans, only a notice about a patriotic parade of university graduates that had taken place the day before. I walked down the prospekt, past the General Staff

Building with its great arch dedicated to the defeat of Napoleon in the War of 1812. Russia had won that war, but Napoleon didn't have hundreds of tanks and bombers to use against us as Germany did. I was eager to go into the General Staff Building and ask where I could enlist in the army, but I knew I should wait until war was declared; otherwise, I might get Andrei into trouble.

Across the street from the General Staff Building was the Hermitage, where I had thought I would be working, and next to it the Winter Palace. Mama had told us in great secrecy how she had once lived in the palace with the daughters of the tsar, when her own mama was lady-in-waiting to the Empress Alexandra. Laughing, she had said, "I splashed around in the tsar's bathtub." All that was long ago, and until that morning I had thought I would have no chance for my own adventures, only day after day of dreary study and work. With talk of a war with Germany, the world was suddenly more exciting. Of course I had seen the worried looks on Andrei's and Mother's faces, but they were old.

On the prospekt, people wandered in and out of the stores. On the bridge across the Griboyadov Canal, a man was selling gaily colored scarves. Reflected in the canal, the brightly painted domes of the Church of the Resurrection were all the colors of the scarves. Seeing a girl walk along with an ice-cream sandwich reminded me it was nearly lunchtime.

Back at the apartment I turned on the radio for a little company while I heated up a pot of cabbage soup. Instead of the news that came on at noon, I heard the word *unimaniye*—"attention." I turned off the fire under the soup and stood listening. The next voice was Comrade Molotov speaking from Moscow. Molotov was deputy premier, just below Stalin himself. I thought, The war is coming.

Molotov spoke in a calm, almost boring voice, as if he were reading the everyday news, but the words sounded in my ears like shouts.

"Men and women, citizens of the Soviet Union," he greeted us, and then he announced that German troops had attacked Russia. German planes had bombed our cities of Kiev and Sevastopol.

My heart was racing. Andrei had been right.

Molotov called for us to rally around "the glorious Bolshevik Party," and around "our great leader, Comrade Stalin."

Why isn't our great leader talking to us now? I wondered. And why did he make us friends with Germany in the first place?

When the speech was over, the radio played patriotic songs. I didn't take the time to pour the soup into a bowl but spooned it lukewarm from the pan. A moment later I was running out of the apartment, still chewing on a crust of bread. I headed back to the General Staff Building, where I marched up the stairway. Before I could enter the building, a guard grabbed my arm.

"Where do you think you are going?"

I took a deep breath. "I heard the radio. We are at war. I want to enlist in the army at once."

I saw the guard holding his lips tightly together to keep from smiling.

Furious, I said, "There is a war. Comrade Molotov said so. Russia needs all the men she can get."

"Men, yes. Not boys. Show me proof you are eighteen and I'll send you to the recruiting office."

I walked away, trying to hold up my head. I knew Mama would never sign anything that said I was eighteen, but maybe Marya would.

I pushed my way through the crowds. I was not the only one who had heard the news. All of Leningrad, like a swarm of bees let loose from its hive, was buzzing into this store and that. There were long lines in front of the State Bank. People left the bank counting their money, worried looks on their faces. Soon they would turn the money into gold and jewelry. We had learned in school what bad things can happen to money when a country is at war.

A woman came out of one of the *gastronom*s, the grocery stores, with a peck of potatoes under one arm and a sack of cabbages under the other. Strung around her throat was a necklace of onions and, poking out of her pocket, a bottle of vodka. When she saw me staring at her, the woman spat angrily at my feet. "Don't come to me for food when you are starving, you idle boy."

I hurried to the Hermitage. I would show the woman who was idle and who was not.

A handwritten sign announced that the museum was closed, but the guard at the door recognized me. "Your sister is in the Dutch gallery. What a terrible thing. Everything here is confusion. Comrade Orbeli is ready to throw himself into the Neva." Comrade Orbeli was the director of the museum. The guard warned, "Everyone is upset. You had better stay away."

I thanked him, and ignoring his advice, I hurried

to the gallery. Marya was balanced on top of a ladder, lifting a picture off the wall, helped by an elderly woman whom I recognized as one of the museum guards. I could see ladders in other galleries and men and women snatching pictures off the walls as if a fire were raging just inches away. There was the sound of pounding and sawing as carpenters hammered together crates.

Marya's blouse was pulled out of her skirt, and her hair was every which way. When she saw me, she said, "Georgi, you are an angel to come so quickly. You've heard the terrible news. Take this Rembrandt from me—and be careful, it's priceless."

I grasped the painting and laid it against the wall. I knew the picture well, for Mama had often brought me to this room. It was *An Old Man in Red*. The man's gnarled, wrinkled hands with their little rivers of blue veins had fascinated me. "Marya, I have to talk with you at once. You need to write something that says I am eighteen."

She gave me a puzzled look. "But you are not yet fifteen."

"Yes, yes, I know that, I'm not a fool, but I'm nearly fifteen, and I want to go into the army."

"Georgi, you are out of your mind. What would Mama say? Anyhow, you need something official. Even if I would do such a thing, and I wouldn't, there is no way I can put words on paper that will get you into the army."

"I have to do something. I won't spend the war mopping floors!"

Marya climbed down the ladder and, reaching up, grabbed me by the shoulders. "You must listen to me for once. Look around you. A room full of Rembrandts, and next door two da Vincis—the greatest artists who ever lived. What if the bombs fall tomorrow? What if they fall on the Hermitage? Room after room of treasures that can never be replaced. There are thousands of such treasures here. You want to save Russia? Here is the best of what Russia has.

Georgi, help me." She was crying.

I imagined a bomb exploding and *An Old Man in Red* crumbling into a thousand pieces. "But where will you put them?"

"We don't know yet. Comrade Orbeli is making arrangements. Our job is to choose what is to go and to pack it. Now give me a hand." She began very carefully to take the painting from the frame.

After that I lost track of time. We went from one gallery to the next. As we took the pictures down, the wooden crates were constructed around them and carefully labeled. I wondered what the pictures must feel, torn from their homes and shut up into boxes.

We emptied the galleries of farmyards with cows and horses, of neat Dutch rooms with everything in place, as if no one lived in them. We packed away picture after picture of kings and empresses and naked ladies. There were hundreds of pictures from the Bible: David with the head of Goliath, Moses with the Ten Commandments, the Holy Family, the return of the prodigal son, and pictures of saints and angels. Stalin had shut all the churches and synagogues but here in the state museum God was everywhere. It made me a little nervous to shut those pictures up in boxes.

Someone brought in sandwiches and tea for us, and we worked on until one in the morning. The sun was low, and there were long shadows on the pavement as we walked home. The prospekt was crowded, as if no one wished to be alone. Several of the stores we passed had signs listing things they were out of. *Leningradskaya Pravda* had put out an extra. The headline was just the one large word: VOINA, war. Still, none of it seemed real to me. "Marya," I asked, "what if the Germans never bomb Leningrad? All our work at the Hermitage will be for nothing." Our backs and arms were aching, and our stomachs were growling with hunger.

For an answer Marya pointed to the covers that had been hastily thrown over the lights of the trolleys to dim them. I noticed that few buildings were lighted. Around us people were looking up at the sky. There, hovering over the General Staff Building like a giant's toy, was an antiaircraft balloon.

CHAPTER THREE

PREPARING FOR BATTLE

June 1941

Early each morning Marya and I headed for the Hermitage. As gallery after gallery was emptied of its treasures, Comrade Orbeli insisted that the empty frames be replaced on the walls.

"It will make it easier to put back the pictures," Marya said, and I could see that in her heart, however long the war took, it would not be over for Marya until the moment the pictures were safely back in their frames.

I was assigned to help in the loading and unloading of the trucks that carted the works of art to railroad cars, which pleased me because I was no longer cooped up in the museum—and besides, it paid more money. Riding on the trucks gave me a chance to see what was going on in the city. It looked as if a mad wizard had waved his wand over Leningrad, turning it into a shabby forest. All the important buildings were cam-ouflaged with green netting. The Party leaders had been quick to think of themselves, for the first nets were cast over the Communist Party headquarters at Smolny. When Mama saw the net, she said, "I wish they would draw the net tight and throw the whole building and all those in it into the Neva. The Party made a bargain with the devil when it joined with Germany, and now it is surprised to see the devil turn on it."

One by one, buildings were erased by the camou-flage nets; even the column with the angel on the square in front of the Winter Palace was draped with netting. When it came to the spire of the Admiralty, everyone was stumped. No one could figure out how to get to the top so that the gold spire, glistening so invitingly in the sun, could be painted out. They even tried to have an antiaircraft balloon drop a rope ladder onto the tower, but nothing worked. It was dangerous to leave it shining there, for the spire would serve as a guidepost for the German bombers.

At first there was no shortage of food, and Mama filled the cupboard. She no longer talked about "not taking more than our share."

"I have been hungry, Georgi, and I know what it's like." She took a part of our savings and bought a *burzhuika*, a little stove that was fired with small pieces of wood. I remembered such a stove in the house in which we had lived in Dudinka when Mama was exiled to Siberia.

"Why do we need a *burzhuika*, Mama, when we already have a stove to cook on and our apartment is heated?"

"That is now, Georgi. Wait and see."

Stranger still was what Mama did with bread. You

could buy as much as you liked, and Mama strung slices on a cord and hung the necklace of slices in a sunny window to dry.

When Olga saw them, she teased Mama. "Who will eat your dried rusks when we have fresh bread to eat?"

Olga was working longer hours, for the radio symphony had been called upon to broadcast patriotic music hour after hour. The Leningrad symphony had been sent out of the city to protect the musicians. The radio symphony in which Olga played was now the city's only orchestra. The musicians had even had a little raise in pay, and with her extra money Olga had bought a new dress and shoes. When she brought them to show us, Mama smiled. "Very pretty, but you will regret those high heels. You had better take them back and exchange them for sturdy shoes or, better yet, food."

"You are a pessimist, Katya," Olga said, and twirled around in her new dress and high heels.

Mama bought sugar and fruit and filled every jar she had with preserves. When the first cabbages were ripe, she put them in a pickling brine.

"The way they did at the Oaks," she said. The Oaks had been my grandmother's country estate, and my mother had told us stories of fields of grain so vast you could not see to the end of them, and a great house that had been burned down during the revolution.

One evening Andrei stopped by. Marya had seen little of him, for he was busy at staff headquarters day and night. We were sitting around the kitchen table listening to the radio. The orchestra was playing the Fifth Symphony by Shostakovich, Russia's great composer who lived right in Leningrad. Marya said, "Olga told me that Shostakovich is working on an important piece that will celebrate Leningrad's victory."

Andrei was no longer the cheerful man he had been. Now he had a troubled face and bad news. "If Shostakovich is writing about a victory, he knows something I don't. There is even a rumor that he is to be flown to Moscow to get him out of danger should the Germans march into the city."

"Andrei," Mama said, "surely it's not as bad as that?"

"Yes. I'm afraid it is. Our army is retreating everywhere. The eleventh and the eighth armies are coming apart. In some of the units half the men are casualties." Andrei knew of my wish, and now he gave me a warning look. "Count your lucky stars that you are too young to join up, Georgi."

In a frightened voice Marya said, "Andrei, will you have to go to the front?"

"No such luck. Everything is chaos here at headquarters. I am working twenty hours a day trying to find food and ammunition for the soldiers."

"It was the same chaos under the tsar in the Great War," Mama said, "and it led to the revolution. Maybe this war will lead to a change in the government, and this time for the better. I've heard a rumor that political prisoners in the camps are being released to join the army. At least they are getting their freedom."

Andrei nodded. "Yes, it's true, but will they live long enough to enjoy it?"

The next day when when my friend Dmitry and I were walking along the prospekt, I told him what Andrei had said. He wouldn't believe me.

"Look, here." He shoved an article in *Leningradskaya Pravda* under my nose. "It says right here in the newspaper that the Russian army is turning back the Germans."

"That's how much you know. You're stupid to believe what the newspaper says." I remembered too late that Dmitry's brother Vladimir was a reporter for the paper.

"You're not patriotic!" Dmitry shouted. "What can you expect from someone whose parents were enemies of the people and exiled to Siberia?"

I hit him on the nose. He hit me back. I felt a loose

tooth, and there was blood on my fist. I don't know what would have happened next, but suddenly, all around us, we saw people running. I think we were glad of an excuse to stop the fight and began to run after them. They were headed for the Admiralty.

"They're going to climb the tower," someone shouted.

For days there had been rumors that several mountain climbers were going to make the attempt to camouflage the Admiralty tower. Their pictures appeared in *Leningradskaya Pravda*. One of the climbers was a music teacher, Fersova. "Why, I know her!" Yelena had said. "She's a friend of Mama's."

Now it was going to happen. Half of the city watched the mountain climbers make their slow way up the tower. We were all holding our breath. When at last they reached the top, we all let out a cheer. The climbers took out paintbrushes and began to cover the bright gold with dark paint. When they were safely down, everyone breathed a sigh of relief, but I couldn't help but be sad that the shining gold that had brightened the city's sky for so long had disappeared.

Our fight was forgotten, and Dmitry and I continued down the prospekt with some idea of looking to see what ships were docked. Dmitry didn't apologize, but he bought two ice creams on a stick and gave me one. We sat at the river's edge eating our ice cream.

"Vladimir is going to the front," Dmitry said. "He's going to be a war correspondent."

I understood why I had made him angry. Even if his brother wasn't a soldier, Dmitry was worried about his brother going off to war. "He'll write the truth," I said, trying to be polite.

"But they won't print it," Dmitry said, trying to be honest.

While I was stuck at the Hermitage, everyone else appeared to be going off to the war. In spite of what he had said, Andrei was transferred to the front, and for days Marya went about with a gloomy face. Sometimes I would awaken in the middle of the night to find her sitting at the kitchen table with a glass of tea.

In spite of his old age, Viktor was also going off to the front. A call had gone out for volunteers. The German army was moving rapidly north. Thousands of workers were needed to dig a last line of defense to keep the armies from crossing the Luga River. Once they crossed the Luga, which was less than a hundred miles from Leningrad, the German army could join with the Finns and make a circle around Leningrad. Except for Lake Ladoga on the northeast, we would be ringed around, closed in as surely as if a fence encircled us—no food or help could come in, and we could not escape. We would be rats in a trap.

"They'll never get past the Luga," Viktor said. "Thousands are going down there to dig ditches and build hills to keep the tanks out. You'll see." He marched off with the others, with Olga running after him to give him his carpet slippers and a bottle of wine.

Even those with jobs were expected to put in three hours of patriotic work each day. Mama chose to unload wood from the barges coming from Finland, although the barges were bringing less and less. The people of Finland hated Russia for invading their country and taking it over. When they saw our soldiers marching south to stop the advancing German army, leaving Finland undefended, the Finns saw a chance to rebel against their old enemy, Russia.

At first I argued with Mama, for unloading the barges was heavy work, especially after a day at the hospital, but each day she brought home a stick or two concealed in her jacket. The small sticks were piled neatly in the kitchen next to the little *burzhuika*. "For the day they are needed," Mama said.

For my three hours of patriotic work I joined Dmitry and hundreds of others digging air-raid shelters in the Summer Garden. Though our hands were covered with blisters and our backs ached, Dmitry and I took to the tunneling like moles. I had a daydream that one of the soldiers who oversaw the work would tap me on the shoulder and say, "Such a hard worker should be in the army, never mind how old you are. There is a place for you." It never happened.

Something even more remarkable happened. One

afternoon as we were flinging dirt over our shoulders, we noticed a small, neatly dressed man with glasses handling the shovel as if he had no idea what a shovel was for. While I thrust my foot against my own shovel and pried it into the hard earth, the man hardly made a dent in the ground. When he saw me staring at him, he gave me a smile so apologetic, I could not resist going over to him with a view to showing him how to angle the shovel and how to force it into the ground with a little help from his foot.

"I'm afraid I am useless at this," he said. He was looking at his hands, which were soft and white and now covered with cruel blisters.

"Look—make your foot do the work, and that will save your hands." I slammed my foot against the shovel to give him a lesson.

"Ah, so that's the way," he said, and tried it out with his own shovel.

There was something familiar about his face. "*Prastitye*, I beg your pardon, but what work did you do before the war?" I asked.

"I work a little with music," he said, and turned back to his shovel.

I looked at him again and turned beet red. It was Dmitry Shostakovich, the great composer.

"*Prastitye, prastitye,*" I mumbled. "I had no idea." I couldn't keep myself from asking, "What are you doing here?"

"I tried to get into the army, but my eyesight kept me out."

"I know how you feel," I said. "With me it's my age."

By now several people had recognized him. They began to crowd around us. Shostakovich looked nervously about and then, clasping his shovel, hurried away.

When I went back to Dmitry, he asked, "Who was that funny little man?"

"That funny little man was just the greatest composer in Russia."

Dmitry refused to believe me. In the early evening, as we left the Summer Garden, I saw Shostakovich from a distance. He was using his foot to good effect.

Dmitry grinned. "There is your great composer," he said. "Now will you admit you made a mistake? What would Shostakovich be doing with a shovel?"

Olga believed me at once. "Yes, I have heard he has worked as an air-raid warden and is now working as a laborer, but every minute he is away from his piano and his desk is a terrible waste."

"He wants to do his part," I said.

"He is writing a great symphony for our city. That is work enough. Why should he dirty his hands?"

Olga was so upset, I said nothing more, but I understood what he was doing. It must have been very lonely for him there in his study. He was writing about Leningrad, and he wanted to be a part of the city.

Though I looked each afternoon, I never saw Shostakovich again. I guessed that some officials felt the way Olga did and the composer was confined to his study.

It was impossible to recognize the Summer Garden

as the same place where only weeks before I had chased Yelena among the trees. There were ugly piles of dirt from the air-raid excavations, the fountains were boarded up, and the statues had been taken down and laid to rest under the ground like so many dead people. The rose garden and flower beds had been torn out by their roots to make the shelters. It was no longer a garden but a muddy scene of destruction. The shelters we were building were to protect us, but the craters we were digging made the Summer Garden look like it had already been bombed. And not only the Summer Garden, but all the parks.

The beauty of the city was gone. The bronze horses on the Anichkov Bridge were underground, and saddest of all, *The Bronze Horseman*, the impressive statue of Peter the Great, had been covered with sandbags. In school we had all learned Pushkin's poem *The Bronze Horseman* and its terrible story of the Leningrad flood of 1824, with coffins from the graveyards floating in the streets. When I told Yelena the poem scared me to death the first time I read it, she said, "A sign of a great poem."

With its buried statues, its camouflage nets and gray paint, and its ruined parks, I no longer recognized my city. As I always did when I was discouraged, I took my worry to Yelena. Somehow she always found a way to cheer me. "How," I asked her, "will Leningrad ever to be the same again?"

For an answer she wrote a poem.

> *Seed the earth with people*
> *burrowing beneath the ground,*
> *in air-raid shelters,*
> *in trenches,*
> *with spring will come*
> *the resurrection.*

I guess she meant eventually everything would be all right, only it looked to me as if it might take a while.

CHAPTER FOUR

MARYA LEAVES

July 1941

Yelena's patriotic work took place on the roof of the Winter Palace, where she worked for three hours each night as an air-raid warden. Though German Messerschmitts sometimes flew over the city, they flew at very high altitudes. As yet there were no bombs, but they could come at any time, and the city had to be prepared. I hated the idea of Yelena risking her life every night, but she was proud of her assignment.

"You are digging air-raid shelters, Georgi, and I will warn everyone when to go into them. You will protect the people, and I will protect the buildings."

"A building isn't worth a life. Promise me you will get down and into the safety of a shelter if the planes come."

She wouldn't promise. "There are thousands and thousands of girls like me in Leningrad," she said, "but there is only one Winter Palace. Come and see for yourself, Georgi."

"There are hundreds of palaces," I argued. And to myself I said, But there is no one like you. Still, I agreed to join her one night after my digging was over. I was eager to see the palace where long ago my mama had lived with the empress and the tsar and their children. She had told Marya and me stories of ballrooms with golden ceilings and a room whose walls were made of precious stone.

"Mama," I said, "I'm going with Yelena tonight to the Winter Palace. Would you like to come with us?"

Mama smiled sadly. "I'd give a great deal to visit the Winter Palace I remember, but not today's Winter Palace." In a hushed voice she said, "There was a great deal of injustice when the tsar lived there, Georgi, but it was spoiled for me when the Bolsheviks took it over. They planned the arrests and murders of thousands of people there. I have no wish to see it again." After a moment Mama relented, for her anger never lasted long, burning and then cooling just as quickly. "Of course you must go with Yelena. She's a brave girl, and whatever has happened in the palace, the building itself must not be blamed. It has always been one of the glories of St. Petersburg."

The roof of the palace stretched for acres, so Yelena was only one of many air-raid wardens assigned to the roof. To reach Yelena's section, we went through door after door and climbed stairway after stairway. The part of the palace we traveled through was unoccupied. I gasped at what I saw: gilded walls, ceilings painted with cupids flying about in blue sky and pink clouds, marble columns, and floors so shiny you could see your reflection in them. Though the crystal chandeliers and all the valuable furniture and paintings had been put away, I could still imagine them as Mama had described them.

The great empty rooms of the palace were so eerie, to break the tension I let go of Yelena's hand and, taking off my shoes, began to slide about over a polished floor. At first Yelena was shocked, but after a moment she slipped out of her shoes, and the two of us glided back and forth, trying to see who could slide the longest distance. When we heard one of the guards coming, we hurriedly got into our shoes and, laughing, raced up the stairway.

At each roof station there were pails of water and sand as well as a wicked-looking ax. I tried to imagine Yelena flailing about with the ax.

"I've tried it, Georgi. It's heavy, but if I had to, I know I could do it."

Yelena's section looked northwest across the Neva to Vasilevsky Island. We settled comfortably against one of the chimneys. Though it was night, a pale sun gilded the Neva. In the sky there was nothing more dangerous than a few pink clouds. The palace was only four stories high, yet we looked down on the green roofs of Leningrad, with their hundreds of chimneys, like so many mushrooms springing up from a forest floor. More than two hundred years ago Peter the Great had built a city where there had been nothing but marshes and sea. When it was finished, he ruled that no building could be taller than his palace.

"Up here on the roof we are like kings and queens," Yelena said, "looking out over our kingdom."

Across the Neva was the camouflaged spire of the Peter and Paul Fortress, and on Vasilevsky Island the university buildings.

Yelena said, "With the war it looks like we will never be students at the university, Georgi. Still, it's nice to think about, like keeping yourself from freezing in the cold by imagining what it would be like to walk into a warm room."

"What would you study at the university?" I asked.

"Russian literature," she said. "I want to read Pushkin and Lermontov and every Russian poem that has ever been written."

I looked around nervously. I didn't want anyone to overhear Yelena if she was going to recite Lermontov, since she always recited his love poetry.

But she only asked, "Georgi, what will you study if the war ends?"

"I want to go back to Siberia," I said. Quickly I added, "Not to Dudinka and the cold and the exile, but to the Siberia Marya and I saw in the summer, the birch trees and the great river and the reindeer and, most of all, the Samoyed people who were so good to us. The Communist Party has shut them and their reindeer up in farms. The Samoyeds must hate it. I want to study the native peoples of Russia—I want to become an expert and convince the Party to let the Samoyeds and their reindeer roam free. We still have the boots and parka they made for my father. I'll show them to you sometime."

Across from Vasilevsky Island were Petrograd Island and the Lenfilm movie studio where all the famous movies were made.

"Maybe I'll write a great film," Yelena said, "like *Ivan the Terrible*."

"And I'll play Ivan."

So we sat talking for three hours in the twilight of the white night. At midnight the next shift arrived, and we made our way back down the stairs and through the empty palace rooms with their ghosts of the dead tsar and empress and their poor dead son and daughters.

Because of staying up so late, I was half asleep the next morning when I reached the Hermitage. Marya was already there. Although some of the museum employees had left for the army and some had been sent off, like Viktor, to the Luga River to build fortifications against the Germans, Comrade Orbeli had managed to recruit new workers. One trainload of the museum's treasures had already left with hundreds of crates. As I had loaded them onto the railroad cars I couldn't help but notice the antiaircraft guns mounted on the cars like giant nursemaids to watch over their charges.

Now the second shipment was nearly ready. There was little left in the museum, only the empty frames. While I was packing one of the last boxes, a soldier wandered into the gallery. Vera, one of the guards, hurried to stop him, calling, *"Ostanovka!"* "Halt!"

Embarrassed, the soldier stopped in his tracks. *"Prastitye,"* he mumbled. "I am from the country and have never been in Leningrad. When our company passed through the city, I wanted a look at the great museum. We learned about it in our school. *Prastitye,"* he said again, and turned to leave.

"That's all right, Vera," I said. With the way the war was going, the soldier might never get to the museum again. "Since you've come this far," I told him, "I'll give you a tour."

The soldier looked around the gallery, disappointed and puzzled. "The frames are all empty."

"Never mind, I packed every painting in this room, and I know them like the back of my hand. All Dutch, every one. There, for example." Guessing what would be sure to interest him, I pointed to an empty gold frame. "That is a picture of a Dutch farm. You can see a man at his spring plowing. He has two big white horses. They look strong enough to pull the whole country to another place on the map, great muscly fellows."

The soldier was staring hard at the empty frame, nodding his head. "Very few trees," I went on, "only one or two starting to bud out. Holland is built on the sea, so you don't have a lot of trees. And in the background the steeple of a church. Over on the right-hand side is a windmill. The Dutch have to spend their lives pumping away the sea. The best thing of all is the sky. In all these paintings it's the finest thing. Holland is flat, so you get as much sky as you want, miles of it.

The painters make the most of it. This one is filled with rosy clouds spread like sour cream on a dish of borscht so that just a bit of the beet juice seeps through."

He looked from the frame to me and back again, nodding eagerly. "Yes," he said, "I see it all. We would have given much to have such horses on our collective farm."

I took him from empty frame to empty frame, pointing out in one picture how cleverly the artist had placed the snow over the countryside and in another how everyone in the village, adults and children alike, was skating on the river, and how a fine big brown dog with a patch of white on his chest was on the ice.

When he left, the soldier took my hand in his and shook it vigorously. "Wonderful pictures," he said. "I'll never forget them, and I'll tell the others on the farm when I get back from the front. Especially the big horses."

That night there was borscht for dinner, and it

reminded me of the farmer-soldier who had come to the gallery. Marya laughed at my story, but I knew she hadn't really listened to me. I guessed she had something she wanted to say to us. I could always tell, because she bit at her lip and peeked out at you from under her dark lashes.

Mama knew it as well. When I finished my tale, Mama said, "Marya, something is on your mind."

In one long breath the words tumbled out. "It is Comrade Orbeli. He has assigned me to travel with the train this time when the last shipment from the Hermitage leaves. Several of us are going, for there must be people at the other end who know how to preserve the treasures. It can't be too damp or too dry for them or they will be ruined. Only I hate to be away from Leningrad. I don't want to leave you, Mama, and if I go, Georgi is sure to do something foolish."

With great indignation I threw my napkin at her, yet the truth was I was shaken by the idea that she would leave us. I had never been separated from Marya; without her I might be in an orphanage or lie buried someplace in Siberia.

"How long will you be gone, dear?" Mama asked. Her face was pale, but her voice was strong. Better than anyone, she knew that you could not say no to an order.

"I don't know, Mama. They won't tell us or perhaps they don't know. It could be months—or longer. It depends on the war."

"Where are you to go?"

From habit Marya lowered her voice. "That's the worst part of it. It's a secret. No one has been told."

"*I* know," I said.

Marya stared at me. "Don't be so smart. Of course you don't know. *I* don't know."

"But I *do* know. When we were loading the first train, I got to talking with the engineer—about how fast the train could go and so forth. He told me the train was going to Sverdlovsk. You'll be safe enough from the Germans there."

Marya's brown eyes were very round. She whispered, "Georgi, you shouldn't have said that."

Mama began to sob. We both looked at her with alarm. Suddenly I realized what I had done, I and my bragging and my big mouth. The city far away in the Ural Mountains that was now called Sverdlovsk was once called Yekaterinburg, which meant the Empress Catherine's City. Like all names in Russia that had anything to do with tsars or empresses, the name had been changed, but to Mama Yekaterinburg stood for hell itself. It was in that city that the Bolsheviks had murdered the tsar and the empress and their son and four daughters, the four daughters who had been like sisters to Mama.

"No, Marya!" Mama said. "You can't go to that terrible place. It's cursed. I'll never see you again."

Marya put her arms around Mama. "Mama, I have to go. Not only is it an order that I mustn't disobey, but those paintings are everything to me. They are like my children. I must go with them."

"Not there, not there," Mama whispered.

"That was long ago," Marya pleaded.

"In my heart it was only a minute ago," Mama said, but she wiped the tears from her eyes. She sighed. "You are right, Marya. When all of this is over, whether we are still here or not, those treasures will be there to remind people what the war was all about. In Germany they are burning paintings. Here we are risking our lives to save them."

The next day, with many kisses and promises to write, Marya left, her last words to me: "Take care of Mama, Georgi, and stay out of trouble."

CHAPTER FIVE

DEFENDING THE CITY

August 1941

The second week in August Viktor returned. Olga had knocked on our door on a warm Saturday evening. "Let me sit for a while with the two of you. It's too hot to sleep, and I worry about Viktor and about Yelena perched on top of the Winter Palace like a dove on a treetop. What if the Germans begin to bomb?"

Olga often knocked on our door. She could not stand to be alone. When there was no one in the apartment with her, we heard the radio going long into the night. I could only guess what voices inside her she was drowning out. I knew Mama was tired after a long day at the hospital as well as the work of unloading wood, but she never turned Olga away.

"I'll put on the kettle," she said. Mama believed that hot tea on a hot night would cool you off.

Suddenly Olga sprang from her chair. "What is that?"

Mother took the hissing kettle from the stove, and we all listened. I heard nothing, but Olga ran to the door and opened it. Someone was calling her name. We followed her to the stairway, and at the bottom of the stairs was Viktor.

"Olga, help me," he cried. We all ran down the stairway, and with me on one side and Mama on his other side and Olga behind pushing, we half carried Viktor up the stairway and into our apartment, where he fell into one of the chairs.

If I had seen him on the street, I don't think I would have recognized him. He had lost half his weight. His cheeks were sunken, and he had a straggly white beard that didn't match his dark hair. He was always a neat man, with his hair slicked back, and though he had only two shirts, the one he wore was always clean. Now his clothes were covered with dirt, and there were streaks of dirt across his face.

He looked and looked at Olga and Mama and me. "Ah, I did not think to ever see you again," he cried. "The Germans have crossed the Luga River. Everything is lost. There were hundreds of thousands of us. We dug trenches until our arms could no longer lift a pick or a shovel, and then we crawled on the ground and dug with our hands. There was hardly any food, and no place to sleep but the fields. All the while, the Germans fired their artillery at us and dropped bombs on us from their planes. A woman who was working beside me was killed. One minute she was there and the next minute . . ." He put his hands over his eyes.

"In the end none of our work mattered. The German tanks rolled over our earthworks as if they were cotton wool. Half our solders didn't have guns, while the Germans were shooting with cannons. We turned and ran, everyone ran. The roads were so crowded, you could hardly move. And not just the volunteers. The soldiers were running as well. The people on the farms were running, driving their farm animals ahead of them. It was like a thousand Noah's arks. And I'll tell you something else. There were Estonians who joined up with the Germans to fight us. Now we must wait for the Germans to put an end to us."

Olga sobbed while Viktor talked, but Mama was busy. She put a glass of tea and a bowl of soup in front of Viktor, who began to throw the food down his throat.

Mama laid a hand on his arm. "Gently, gently, Viktor. You will make yourself sick."

"The Germans will march into Leningrad and kill us all," Olga wailed.

"No," Mama said. "They will think there is no need for that. They will surround us, hoping to starve us, and only then will they march into the city. That way they won't have to sacrifice their soldiers."

"But they will bomb us." Olga began to cry again.

"It's all over," Viktor said. His soup bowl was empty, and some color was coming back to his face.

I couldn't stand such talk. "Why is everyone giving up?" I demanded. "We have bomb shelters now, and we are going to learn how to fight the Germans hand-to-hand if we have to."

"Georgi is right," Mama said. "This is our city. Why should we let the Germans take it from us? You will see. When the time comes, we'll know how to fight."

The next day the headline in the newspaper read, THE ENEMY IS AT THE GATES. When I went to the food store for Mama to get flour, I found long lines of angry people. Word had gotten out that the German army had crossed the Luga. Everyone was thinking the same thing: The Germans will starve us.

At once the government passed out ration cards. We were allowed a little over a pound of bread a day, and if you got to the store in time, there was sugar and fat and millet to make porridge. We even had bread left over for Mama to slice and dry into her rusks. Our rusk bag was bursting at the seams, but still Mama dried the bread.

Large numbers of women and children were sent out of the city, but so many refugees flooded into Leningrad from the south to escape the Germans, the population of the city stayed at three million. Rumors flew. There was a story that German planes dropped leaflets on the outskirts of the city, telling the women to put on white dresses so that the bombers could see them and not drop bombs near them. Some women were foolish enough to do it, and instead of sparing the women, the German bombers used the white spots as targets.

Leningrad was divided into sections, several blocks to a section. Each one of the city's 150 sections was to be protected by an army of volunteers. Everyone was welcome. At last I was to be in an army, but such an army: women, children, and old men. Each section had its own store of ammunition. Heavy guns were put onto trucks. The trucks would be driven about to be used where they were needed. We collected bottles and were taught how to make bombs and throw them against tanks. We also practiced using rifles so that we could shoot down Germans parachuting into the city. There were not enough rifles for each of us to have one to practice with, just one rifle that was passed around within our section. I had never fired a gun before, and when my turn came to try the rifle, I nearly fell over from its recoil.

To stop the German tanks from advancing into Leningrad, cement blocks were scattered throughout the city, making it look like a giant had spilled sugar cubes. Wooden posts were pounded into any open space—parks, squares, and even the cemeteries—to keep Germans from parachuting into the city. Everyone who could lift a shovel or a pick was put to work. Thousands of miles of ditches were plowed to stop the German tanks. The ditches hadn't stopped the Germans at the Luga River, but that didn't seem to matter.

One day a burly soldier marched into our section and called for volunteers to demonstrate how to kill a German soldier if one happened to walk down one of Leningrad's streets. Dmitry and I volunteered at once. The soldier started his lesson with me.

"Go ahead and try to hit me," the soldier ordered.

I swung at his chin, and before my fist could connect, I was propelled into the air and landed on the sidewalk.

Dmitry cheered. The soldier gave him a stony look and the same order. In a minute he was beside me on the ground while the others applauded.

All morning we were instructed on how to dispose of German soldiers, and all afternoon Dmitry and I practiced on each other until we were black and blue. After that we were careful in patrolling our section, eager to come upon the enemy so that we could put our new skills into practice, but we saw no German soldiers.

At the end of August Dmitry's reporter brother, Vladimir, returned from the front with more bad news, so bad it could not be kept out of the newspaper. The headline read: VIRONA LOST. The *Virona* had been one of the navy's largest ships. Vladimir had been covering the war with the Russian navy in the Gulf of Finland. The ships were anchored near the city of Tallinn on the coast of Estonia, another country that Russia had conquered. I begged Dmitry to let me come and hear Vladimir's story for myself.

The Trushins' apartment was a pleasure to visit. Mrs. Trushin always seemed to be covered with flour. No sooner did you poke your head inside their place than Mrs. Trushin would open the oven door and take out some *piroshki* or *makivneki* oozing raisins, which was probably why all the Trushins were a little on the chubby side. The minute I walked through the door of the apartment, I could smell fresh baking. There were no raisins to be had now, nor meat for *piroshki*, but still there was a wonderful fragrance.

"Georgi, come and have some egg bread," Mrs. Trushin said. "I baked it for poor Vladimir. What he has been through! Let me pour you some tea, and here are the sugar cubes. It's a miracle I could still find some."

The Trushins drank their tea in the old-fashioned way, holding a cube of sugar in their mouths to sweeten the tea as it went down.

I joined Dmitry, Vladimir, and Mr. Trushin, who worked in the warehouses of the freight docks. The warehouses were where food was stored. Whether Mr. Trushin was able to fill his pockets I never knew, but there were always plenty of ingredients for Mrs. Trushin's baking.

Mr. Trushin said, "Vladimir is telling us the sad story of the Russian navy. I'd like to know who was stupid enough to send our navy away from the safety of the Kronstadt naval base." Kronstadt was on an island about thirty miles east of Leningrad.

"The deed is done, Papa," Vladimir said. "What good does it do to talk about who is to blame? If you had seen what I saw, none of that would matter to you." Vladimir was unshaven, his hair long, his clothes a mixture of army and navy castoffs.

"Vladimir was on the *Virona*," Dmitry said proudly.

"We never had a chance," Vladimir said. "The Germans guns were only a few miles away, and their shells came one after another. Overhead, German Junkers were dropping bombs on us. There must have been nearly two hundred boats there, all of them sitting ducks. Before they sailed away, the ships were supposed to take on board all the Russians from Estonia who were trying to leave the country to escape the Germans. On the *Virona* we had the Russian navy families who had been stationed there.

"It wasn't just the the shelling and the bombing," Vladimir went on. "A terrible storm blew up, and once we were under way, we had to make our path through the German mines."

I knew all about mines. "They're magnetic, aren't they? They're drawn to the metal in the ships."

"Everybody knows that," Dmitry said.

"Those mines made us inch along. Still, we sat down to dinner as if we were in Mama's kitchen. Afterward I went up on deck to watch the shelling and the bombs. It was like a great fireworks display, the German shells and bombs and our own antiaircraft guns on the ship booming away at the planes. All at once the ship exploded under me. In one second I was in the air, and then I was in the cold bathtub. People were swimming all around me, calling out for help. I kicked off my shoes and treaded water until I spotted a plank from the ship. I hung on for dear life."

Mrs. Trushin was wiping tears from her eyes with one hand and making the sign of the cross with the other. She urged more egg bread and tea on Vladimir. "You must eat, my darling, to get your strength back."

"A cutter picked me and several others up, but many were drowned. Of the twenty-nine Russian transports that set sail, twenty-three were lost."

"The fleet should never have been cooped up there in reach of the Germans," Mr. Trushin said. "What were the commanders thinking?"

"In this country," Vladimir said with a shrug, "if you think for yourself, they shoot you."

"Vladimir!" Mrs. Trushin said. "How can you say such a thing?"

"I say it to you because I can say it to no one else."

"But what does it mean?" I wanted to know.

"It means," Vladimir said, "that the Germans are drawing the noose more tightly around Leningrad."

I had to hurry through the streets to reach home, for a ten-o'clock curfew was now in effect. There had been almost no bombing in Leningrad. Still, listening to Vladimir, I worried more than ever about Yelena sitting up on the roof of the palace. I needn't have worried, for when I got home, I found Yelena and

Olga looking out for me.

"Wonderful news!" Olga greeted me from the top of the stairway. "They have put antiaircraft guns on the roof of the palace, and the soldiers are on guard there. Yelena was sent home."

"Georgi, come inside our apartment and listen," Yelena said. "Anna Akhmatova is going to be on the radio. Your mother is already in our kitchen."

Viktor had recovered and was now on air-raid duty, so we were only four sitting around the table. Akhmatova was Leningrad's most famous poet. One by one she had seen poets silenced. Her dearest friend, the great poet Osip Mandelstam, had been arrested right before her eyes. He had died in a prison camp. Akhmatova's husband had been executed by the Bolsheviks. After that, her poetry was banned in the Soviet Union. Now here she was, reading her poems on the radio.

I knew all about Akhmatova because she was Yelena's hero. I had complained that poets were useless in a war, but Yelena had told me that it was as important to feed the spirit of the city as it was the city's hunger. "Akhmatova's words do that," Yelena said. Yelena and some poet friends of hers at the library were printing poems and placing them around the city for people to read.

In her strong voice Akhmatova greeted the citizens of the city. Leningrad had always been a part of her life, she said. "Leningrad gave my poetry its spirit." Leningrad, she promised, would never be conquered by the Germans.

Yelena and Olga were crying; even Mama had tears in her eyes. For once I was glad I wasn't in the army. I was in Leningrad, and Leningrad was sure to be as dangerous a place as any battlefield.

CHAPTER SIX

SPIES

September 1941

Dmitry and I patrolled our section of Leningrad carefully, for rumors were flying about that there were German spies in the city. One evening after supper, as we were walking down the Nevsky Prospekt, we noticed a man taking pictures. He photographed the old Straganov Palace, the Kazan Cathedral, and a bookstore. Dmitry and I looked at each other and back at the man. He was dressed in an old overcoat, much too big for him. His long white hair straggled out from beneath a little peaked cap.

"I've never seen such a cap," I said. "It looks foreign."

"German," Dmitry whispered.

"He's taking pictures so the Germans know what to bomb," I said.

We followed the man, keeping just behind him and pausing in the shelter of a storefront while he took a picture. He was photographing the Gostiny Dvor, a collection of stores and stalls.

Dmitry whispered, "We should report him."

"By the time the police get here, he could be gone," I said. "We should make a citizen's arrest."

Dmitry didn't look too happy. "What if he shoots us?"

"There are two of us and only one of him. One of us can go for the camera and the other for his gun."

"I'll get the camera," Dmitry said.

I was beginning to feel a little doubtful. "First we'll ask him what he's doing."

As he raised his camera to photograph the Anichkov Palace, I confronted him. "You are taking photographs for the bombing."

"Yes, yes, now get out of my way. You have

already spoiled a perfect shot and film is scarce."

It was all the confirmation we needed. Dmitry and I struck. Dmitry grabbed the man's camera and I wrapped my arms around him, getting a stranglehold so that he couldn't reach for a gun.

The man fought back, kicking at my shins and butting Dmitry with his head. At the top of his voice he screamed, "Thieves! Thieves!"

A crowd began to gather. "Keep him from escaping!" I shouted. "He's a German spy!"

At the same time, he was yelling at the crowd, "Thieves! Get a policeman!"

Much to my relief, a policeman appeared, but instead of taking the spy into custody, he grabbed me and Dmitry, who was holding the spy's camera.

"He'll get away," I said to the policeman.

"These hoodlums have stolen my camera," the man said.

"But he admitted he was taking pictures of everything so the Germans would know what to bomb," I insisted. "He said so."

"I said nothing of the kind. I am Josif Vasilyevich Vronsky of the Leningrad Historical Society. I have been commissioned by the society to photograph all of our famous landmarks in the event there is damage from bombs. We must know how to reconstruct the buildings." He was fumbling in his pockets and now drew out a leather case, from which he extracted his identification papers.

"Will you press charges?" the policeman asked Vronsky, handing back his camera.

Vronsky looked at us. I think he must have seen in our faces our bewilderment and how embarrassed we were. He began to laugh. *"Nichevo,"* he said to the policeman. "It is just a misunderstanding. I have no time to waste in a police station." He turned to us. "The next time you go spy hunting, use the sense God gave you, or all the citizens of the city will end up in jail."

Red-faced, we slunk away, trying not to hear

the laughter of the crowd.

The next day Dmitry reported that Vladimir had gone off on another assignment to the front. Dmitry didn't know where, but he whispered that he thought it was north toward Finland. "The dirty Finns have joined up with the Germans. Vladimir says they are nearly to our northern border."

"If we hadn't invaded their country, maybe they would have been with us instead of against us," I said.

At first Dmitry looked like he was going to start another fight, but then he only shrugged. After our spy mistake a lot of the fight had gone out of us.

The Germans and the Finns were to the north, and to the west there was the Gulf of Finland with all the German navy. One day we were shocked to hear the sound of cannons firing into the city from the south. There was still Lake Ladoga on the northeast of the city, but our hopes were pinned to the southeast, where the railroad ran from Leningrad to Moscow. Our hope gave out, for on the very day we heard the cannons, the Germans parachuted into the city of Mga and cut off the railroad. My first thought was of Marya. How would she get back?

"We are like rats in a trap," I said to Dmitry. "The circle is complete."

Now that they had us encircled, the bombing grew worse. Leningrad's famous roller coaster, the *Amerikanskaya gora*, went up like like a box of matches. The zoo was bombed, and we could hear the pitiful cries of the animals. Yelena and Olga were horrified and crouched inside with their hands over their ears. Marya and I had ridden on the roller coaster and spent afternoons in the zoo. All that was over.

It was on the fourth of September, two days before my fifteenth birthday, when the great tragedy happened, changing the lives of everyone in the city. Mama and I were reading a letter from Marya. The postmark had been blacked out, and even though we knew she was somewhere in the city of Sverdlovsk, Marya was not allowed to send a return address. She said she was well and wished she could send food our way. "My children are safe," she said, and we knew she meant the treasures from the Hermitage.

As we were reading the letter, I happened to glance out the window. The whole sky was exploding in a firestorm. We ran out onto the balcony. The people on the prospekt were looking to the southwest side of the city, where flames were rising. Mama said what I had been too afraid to say aloud.

"God help us. They have bombed the food warehouses."

It was true. The whole of the city's supply of food was being destroyed—all the sugar, flour, butter, and meat. All gone. The faces of the people on the street below us were a frightening red from the reflection of the flames. We were all coughing, for the smoke had settled like a suffocating blanket over the city. That morning there had been enough food for the city. By the evening we were all facing starvation.

The next day we learned the terrible results of the

bombing. With the smoke still covering the city, an announcement was made that our rations would be cut in half. In the past, if you had a little extra money there were stores where you could buy what you needed without ration coupons. No more. When Mama went for a loaf of bread, the bakery was closed. For breakfast I had one of Mama's dried rusks with a little jelly and weak tea. Since the beginning of the war I had been able to eat my fill, but now I was hungry.

Olga knocked on our door. "Katya, what am I to do? Yesterday I traded my ration coupons for a jar of caviar. I know it was wrong, but the conductor of the symphony is cross with us all of the time and caviar always cheers me." She looked longingly at Mama's bag of dried bread rusks, the crock of cabbages in brine, and the row of jellies on our shelf.

"We will help you, Olga, but you must also trade. I will have to do the same," Mama said.

"But I have nothing to trade."

"Nonsense," Mama said. "You have a closet full

of clothes you don't need. You can take those to the outskirts of town, where there are farms, and trade with the peasants for food. I mean to do it myself."

We all trooped into Olga's apartment. Yelena looked surprised. "What will the farm women do with Mother's clothes?"

Mama smiled. "They will turn the dresses into quilts to help them keep warm. The shoes they will take apart and turn the leather into something sensible."

When Olga opened her closet door, it was like one of the paintings in the Hermitage. It looked like a hundred paint pots had been spilled. Hanging up were Gypsy skirts, embroidered blouses, and fringed scarves in rainbow colors. Shoes were heaped up on the closet floor.

"Not this one," Olga said, tenderly holding a silk scarf covered all over with flowers. "I wore it at my first concert. I would never give it up."

Mama swept up the scarf and several others, as well as an armful of shoes. Olga watched, tears in her eyes. "Listen," Mama said. "Soon even the food the peasants have on the farms will be gone—or, worse, we won't be able to get to the farms. What good will these things do you then? Can you eat them?"

Yelena was searching through her own things, adding to the brightly colored heap. I recognized a dress she had worn the first time we had gone out together on our own. We had attended a movie, the great director Eisenstein's *Aleksandr Nevsky*. Yelena had cried when the Russian prince had died. I had tried to comfort her, but she only shook her head and sobbed, "I love pictures that make me cry." I was sorry to see the dress go.

The next morning Olga and Mama left with their packages, and that evening when they returned, Olga proudly showed off sausages, cereal, and dried berries.

"Look, Yelena," she said, "six fresh eggs!" I couldn't help noticing that her beloved flowered scarf was poking out of her pocket.

Viktor, looking hungrily at the eggs, congratulated Olga. "I hear there is still food to be had on the outskirts of the city, where the Germans are bombing," he said. "The farmers left some of the root vegetables in the ground when their houses were destroyed."

I got out our map and asked Viktor to show me where those fields were. Immediately, Mama said, "Georgi, put that map away. Don't even think of going there. I have enough worry without thinking of bombs falling over you."

I took one more quick look at the map and folded it up. Early the next morning I was at the Trushins' apartment, calling for Dmitry. As soon as I walked into their apartment, I noticed something missing. There was no smell of fresh baking. I think until that minute I hadn't really understood what the fire at the food warehouses would mean. Mr. Trushin had just come home. He was black with soot and ashes.

"There is nothing left in the warehouses," he said. "Only a little melted sugar we are trying to scrape up from the ground. Every little bit counts." He sighed. "No more little presents for my dear wife."

"Ivanovich, what are you talking about?" Mrs. Trushin said. "I have the greatest gift of all. *You* weren't burned up in that terrible fire. What a day I had until I saw you, but it's true we will miss the things you brought home. We have nothing but a little kasha and some cabbage, and the stores have nothing."

"I think I know where we can dig up some vegetables," I said, "if Dmitry wants to come with me."

Her face lit up. "What a good boy. How I would like to have some carrots for our soup. Dmitry, you go with Georgi." She found some sacks and a knife for each of us and sent us on our way.

If she had known me the way my mother did, Mrs. Trushin wouldn't have been so quick to send Dmitry with me, but Dmitry knew me. The minute we were outside he said, "What do we have to do to get these vegetables?"

I explained.

"What do you mean, bombs?"

"They're probably not bombing there anymore, since everyone has left."

"Everyone has left because they are smarter than we are," Dmitry said, but he didn't turn back. He was thinking, as I was, that if we could not be soldiers, we could at least have our own adventures.

As we neared the farmland, the artillery grew louder and louder. I looked at Dmitry and he looked at me. Each of us was waiting for the other to turn back, but neither of us wanted to be the first to make a move.

I had been here before. On summer days I had come with Mama and Marya for a day in the countryside. We would bring picnic baskets, and after asking permission from the farmers, we would sit under a tree and have our lunch. The grain would be golden in the fields and cows fat and sleek. Before we returned to the city, we would buy eggs, and milk still warm from the cows. The farms had looked like a child's drawing with a big sun in the sky; now it looked as if someone had taken a black crayon and scratched out the pretty drawing.

It would be quiet for a few minutes, and we would think the shelling was over, but just as we started to relax, there would be a crack like thunder and I could feel the ground shake under me.

As we neared the deserted farms, we began to see more people like ourselves, and we felt a little better. It was unlikely that we all would be killed; some of us at least would escape. The first farmhouse we reached was a burned-out skeleton. The windows were shattered and the roof gone. Two women were digging in the ground, filling sacks. They looked at us as if to say, "We were here first." We turned away.

Every farm was occupied by people from the city with their sacks. If you approached, they stopped their digging and gave you a threatening look. After a bit we came to a farm where there was a terrible smell from a cow that lay dead next to what must have once been a stable. No one was digging there. Dmitry and I took our handkerchiefs and wrapped them around our noses. "They say you get used to bad smells," I said.

"I hope I get used to it before I throw up," Dmitry said.

We spotted the wilted ferny leaves of carrots and began to dig. There were turnips and parsnips in the ground as well. By then we were so hungry, we chewed away at the carrots, no longer caring about the smell or all the dirt we were swallowing. We had almost become used to the shelling and the distant explosions, but we were unprepared for the great clap of thunder as a shell hit close to us and clouds of earth shot up into the sky and then rained down on us. I don't know which one of us ran faster. Sometimes I was ahead and sometimes Dmitry, the sacks slamming against our legs. We were not the only ones running. Everyone was heading for the city.

We made our way through the backstreets, ready, should we be stopped, with a story that we had visited relatives in the country, but no one stopped us. It was nearly dark when I left Dmitry at his house and reached our own apartment. I was sure Mama would be so pleased to have the vegetables that nothing would be said about where I had found them. I should have known Mama better.

"Georgi, where have you been? I've been looking all over for you. I went to the Trushins' and Dmitry was gone as well. They said you were out digging vegetables. Georgi, tell me you didn't go where the bombing was."

I handed her my bulging sack. "They're root vegetables, Mama. They'll last us all winter."

"Do you think I would exchange my son for a bag of turnips?" She looked very angry.

"There are carrots and parsnips as well," I said.

"That makes it better?"

For a minute I thought she was going to pitch the bag out the window, but she only threw her arms around me. A moment later she was pushing me away. "What is that terrible smell? Take a bath at once."

CHAPTER SEVEN

UNDER FIRE

September, October 1941

"Moscow must finally be paying some attention to Leningrad," Viktor said. "They've sent General Zhukov to us. I hear that since the old man came, everyone on the General Staff has been on duty twenty-four hours with no sleep. He's like a dog with a rat between his teeth. He's shaking up the whole General Staff, but whether Moscow sent him to save the city or destroy it, who knows?"

Viktor's words, "save the city or destroy it," took on new meaning. The German shelling of the city and the bombing increased. The German army crept closer and closer to Leningrad. Word was that any day they would enter the city. No one believed that they would be merciful to us.

Olga told us that the composer Shostakovich had left Leningrad. "When there was no electricity, he worked by candlelight on his symphony. He didn't want to leave, but Moscow ordered it. They came and told him to pack up, that it was too dangerous in Leningrad. He says he will be back and that the new symphony will be for our city."

The air-raid shelters were finished, and Dmitry and I had a new assignment. We were given buckets of paint and told to paint over all the street signs in the city. "If the Germans come," we were told, "they won't know where to go."

Dmitry and I looked at each other.

Under his breath Dmitry said, "If the Germans are strolling down our streets, what does it matter whether they know whether to turn left at the Nevsky Prospekt and right at the Ligovsky Prospekt?"

Still, it was an order, and we took the black paint and splashed it about, leaving as much on ourselves as on the signposts. We joked about the signs, but still it was not pleasant to think that General Zhukov expected German soldiers in the city. Worse was to come. We were ordered to the sewers.

We weren't volunteers any longer, but workers in the city's brigades. The officer who commanded our sector of workers told us our job would be crucial in saving the city, which made us feel better until our brigade was marched to one of the entrances of the sewer system. It had never occurred to me that you could actually go where what you flushed down the toilet went. We were all prepared to hold our noses, but as we climbed down the steel ladder into the darkened tunnel beneath, it wasn't so bad.

"It's mostly rainwater from the storm sewers," the officer reassured us. Still we hugged the sides of the walkways. "This far down," the officer said, "it is safe from the German bombs. What we want to do is establish a whole system of communications. Up above you painted out the street signs. Down here we are going to put up street signs. If the city is threatened, we can move guns and ammunition to wherever they are needed."

All that week, armed with maps of the sewer system, we explored the little byways and turnings, working our way slowly from one manhole to another and from one entrance to another and marking them all. It was like a game of hide-and-seek.

At the same time, we discovered, men were wiring all the bridges of the city so that they could be blown up if the Germans marched in. And not only the bridges, but the city's docks, the railway that circled the city, St. Isaac's Cathedral, the General Staff Building, and even the Winter Palace. There was a rumor that the whole Russian navy was to be scuttled, completely destroyed to keep it out of the hands of the Germans. Even the newspaper finally admitted our danger. The headline in *Leningradskaya Pravda* said

LENINGRAD—TO BE OR NOT TO BE?

"Mama," I said, "the whole city will disappear." I knew how much she loved the city.

Usually she managed a smile, no matter how bad the news. Now her face was cold. "Would you have the Germans marching down the prospekt and Hitler giving a speech at Palace Square with the angel looking down? Never."

"Mama, the French let the Germans march down the Champs-Elysées, their main street, rather than destroy the whole city."

"The French have their own priorities and may do as they please," Mama said, and would not say another word.

I remembered the watercolors of St. Petersburg Marya had made for Mama and Papa when we were in Siberia, but this was not the same city. The early-fall weather was mild and the sun like gold, yet the city was ugly. After supper one evening Yelena and I walked along the prospekt. We could hear guns in the distance. To stop the German tanks, there were machine-gun posts and concrete blocks and cruel-looking steel contraptions called hedgehogs because of their bristly steel teeth. Lumber was piled every which way. Everything that could be done to stop the German army from rolling through the city had been done.

"It's as if some witch had put a curse on the city," Yelena said. "I can't even remember what it used to be like."

The Summer Garden where we had had our picnic was nothing but muddy earthworks to protect the air-raid shelters under the garden. The city's buildings were covered with nets; even the sky over our heads was full of ugly barrage balloons like so many buzzards. Only when we stood at the edge of the seawall and looked down at the Neva could we forget the war for a moment.

Yelena said, "Rivers are beautiful, but they are cruel as well. The Neva flows on as it has for thousands of years and will keep flowing on to the sea. It doesn't care one way or the other what happens to the city." She sounded discouraged.

"Is something wrong?" I asked.

"I feel so helpless, Georgi. All I do is sit all day long in the library."

"I know what you mean," I said. "It's the same for me."

"Georgi, you have been out every day. You helped to save the paintings, you dug the air-raid shelters, you are a member of the volunteers, you even risked your life to get food from the farms."

"All that is nothing," I said. I felt as useless as Yelena did.

On the night of September 17 there was a high alert. All of us in the guard were summoned to our posts and told that we would not go home. We were to sleep right there. Dmitry and I were stationed near Palace Square. We were supposed to be armed, but there were not enough guns to go around. Ancient guns were yanked from the walls of the Russian Museum. People brought shovels and brooms.

"The Germans are going to break into the city tonight," Dmitry said. "I feel it in my bones."

It was hard to know what to be most afraid of, the Germans or the whole city going up in one terrible explosion from the dynamite we had set ourselves. There were rumors everywhere: the town of Pushkin had fallen, the railroad that circled the city had been taken by the Germans, the Baltic fleet at the Kronstadt naval base had been scuttled. No one knew the truth. We knew only that in the morning, after sleeping at our posts, we were still alive and Leningrad was still there.

The next day we heard the Germans were within ten miles of Palace Square and only two miles from the great Kirov plant where munitions and tanks were being made. The laborers at the plant worked sixteen hours a day turning out munitions, and then at night they armed themselves and slept at the plant to protect it from the Germans. It was known that if the Germans got any closer, the plant would be blown up.

General Zhukov threatened to kill any soldier who retreated an inch. No one knew where the front was, because where it was a minute ago was not where it was now.

Little by little we learned the truth. The great ship *Marat* had been sunk, but most of the rest of the fleet survived at Kronstadt, their guns aimed at the Germans on the Finnish shore. Pushkin, only fifteen miles away from Leningrad, had been taken by the Germans. This news was terrible for Mama. Pushkin was the name given to Tsar's Village, where Mama had lived in the Alexander Palace, and nearby was the magnificent Catherine Palace, which had been turned into a hospital during the Great War. It was said the Germans were using the Catherine Palace as a stable for their horses.

When she first heard what had happened, Mama said, "Show me, Georgi, what they taught you of hand-to-hand fighting." Mama had a furious look in her eye. "I have a mind to go to Tsar's Village myself and strangle those barbarians."

There was an air raid nearly every evening now. The raids were especially dangerous because the Germans were so close to Leningrad, there was little time to get to the shelters. One minute things were peaceful, and the next moment the planes were dropping their bombs on us. You had to decide if you wanted to take the trouble to go to a shelter. It was miserable squeezed in with a lot of other people. It was too dark to read and too noisy to sleep. Just as the all clear was sounded and you climbed out of the shelter, there was another air-raid warning and back you went.

After a while I just kept on with what I was doing. It was the same with others. If you had been standing for an hour in the bread line at a bakery, you wouldn't want to lose your place. Yet all around you buildings were going up in flames. Walking was always accompanied by a sickening crunch of broken glass.

One day a government building was bombed and all the official papers burned. There was so much paper that the fine ashes drifted over the city for hours, shutting out the sun. Viktor laughed. "I always said the government was all paperwork."

Mama was more serious. "Let's hope they were the records of the next wave of poor unfortunates about to be arrested by the government."

One evening in late September Dmitry pounded on the door. "Come at once—there's a huge bomb near the Erisman Hospital. They're defusing it."

My heart was in my throat. Mama was working late at the hospital that night. I ran after Dmitry, sprinting across the bridge to the Petrograd side, where the hospital was located. When I saw how near to the hospital the bomb was, I could scarcely get my breath. Though I knew the danger, I could not keep from drawing close to watch the men defusing the bomb. Dmitry and I climbed under the rope meant to keep people away. The huge bomb was fifteen feet into the ground.

Someone said, "There's a soldiers' barracks next

to the hospital, full of ammunition. If the bomb goes off, the hospital and everyone in it will go with it." He looked around and smiled. "And ourselves as well."

Dmitry kept pulling on my shirt and urging me to move away, but I was too wrapped up in watching the men to pay attention. When he gave a tug so hard I nearly fell over, I looked up.

"Over there," he said, pointing to the hospital entrance. The hospital was being evacuated. Nurses and orderlies dressed in white were helping patients to leave. I ran over, looking for Mama. When I couldn't find her, I went up to one of the nurses. "I'm looking for Ekaterina Ivanova Gnedich."

The nurse pushed me out of her way, saying over her shoulder, "Ekaterina Ivanova is staying in the hospital with the patients who are too ill to move."

It was nearly time for the curfew, and Dmitry tried to get me to leave.

"No," I said. "Not as long as my mother is in the hospital."

He shook his head and left along with the others.

I was the only onlooker when an officer strode over and grabbed me by the shoulder. "Don't you know there's a curfew on? I'm taking you to the station."

I shook loose. "My mother is a nurse in the hospital, and she's staying there with the sick people. I'm not leaving here until I see the bomb is defused." I didn't care what the officer said.

He looked at me for a long time, and then he took an official piece of paper out of his pocket. "This is a pass," he said. "It will allow you to remain here, but just for the night." With that he turned on his heel and left.

The bomb squad worked all night; the dark hole in which they worked was lit by lanterns, which made the workers' long shadows move with them. By early morning the bomb was defused and the men climbed out of the crater, wiping the dirt and sweat from their faces. The ambulances returned with the evacuated patients and hospital staff. After a half hour or so I saw Mama with two other nurses leaving the hospital. At first I was going to run up to her, but I didn't want her to know I had been there all night, right next to the bomb. Racing down the backstreets, I got to the apartment and pulled the covers over my head before she walked through the apartment door.

At our breakfast of a small hunk of dry bread and a mug of hot water, I asked Mama, "Why did you get home so late?"

"We were shorthanded last night," she said. "What did you do while I was at the hospital?"

"Dmitry and I just did a little sightseeing."

"You shouldn't be on the streets, Georgi. It can be dangerous, what with the bombs."

"What about you, Mama?"

"Oh, you needn't worry about me. The hospital is safe."

October brought the first snow and more bad news. The city of Kiev had fallen, and Moscow was in danger. For us the bombing was worse than ever. Thousands of bombs fell. Our apartment shook as if we were in the midst of an earthquake. All night long you could hear the fire engines racing from one fire to the next. There were burned-out houses and stores on every street. People lost what little they had, and the worst thing you could lose was your ration book. Without it you could get no food. At first the lost ration books were replaced, but people cheated and said they had lost their books when they hadn't, so the government refused to replace them. The unfortunate people who had lost their houses now had no food.

We thought about food all day long. We were allowed only a little over two ounces of bread a day. And what bread it was! Everything they could find went into its making: flaxseed, cottonseed, sawdust, cellulose, and moldy flour. It was all we could do to swallow it. Sometimes we got a morsel of fish, and when there was no more food for the horses remaining in the city, the horses were slaughtered and we had a bit of delicious meat.

Inside the houses there was no heat, for there was no kerosene nor wood, and only an hour of electricity each day. Now Mama proudly brought out her little *burzhuika*, which was so small it could be heated with the pieces of wood she had gathered from the barges. It did not warm us, but its flame was cheering and we could still boil water and warm our hands on the hot glasses that held the water.

There was one bit of good news. Many German tanks had been called away from Leningrad to the outskirts of Moscow, where a battle was going on. For the moment the danger of invading Leningrad was over. General Zhukov was needed in Moscow and left our city to darkness and hunger, but he left it free of Germans.

The new enemy was hunger. It raged about the city like a savage wolf. It was all any of us could think about. We awakened hungry, went to bed hungry. There was no hour of the day when you did not long for food. Yelena and I argued. "Better to eat every crumb of your ration all at once," I insisted, "and be a little satisfied at least once a day."

"No, no," Yelena said. "Better to dole the bread out a little at a time—then there will be something to look forward to."

We tried to outdo each other with imagined meals.

"First," I said, "a fish soup, with big lumps of codfish and potatoes."

"No, Georgi, chicken soup with carrots and leeks and tender little dumplings."

"Boiled beef with pickles."

"Pork paprikash with sour cream."

We always agreed on the dessert—ice cream made with plenty of thick cream and fresh strawberries. After our game we would settle down to our single slice of bread that tasted of sawdust, or there would be a thin soup made from a bit of cabbage and a bone with no meat.

"They had better give me a little more," Olga said,

"or I won't be able to lift my violin."

It was true. Olga, who had been plump, was now thin and drawn. Even the music we heard through the walls of the apartment was weak and, for the first time, sad.

Yelena's dresses hung on her as if she were wearing the hand-me-downs of a much larger sister. Most frightening of all was Viktor. His face had been carved away by hunger. His eyes were sunken and there were craters where his cheeks had been. Mama ate at the hospital canteen, but she couldn't have eaten much, for she brought home bits of bread and lumps of potato concealed in her purse. I would not eat her hoardings but passed them on to Olga and Yelena.

Yelena was still working in the library. "Hundreds of thousands of our rarest books have been sent away for safekeeping. "The people are coming to us with such sad questions. They want to know how to make jelly from glue and how to make a soup from a leather belt."

"Doesn't anyone come in to read?"

"Yes, more than ever. There's no heat, but they come wrapped in their coats and look for a table where a bit of warm sunshine comes in through the window. They read books about faraway places where the sun shines and food hangs from trees, but we have to be careful about lending books or there would be none left. People take them home and burn them as fuel for their stoves." She looked truly horrified.

Cold was added to hunger. When you went to bed at night, you wore as many clothes as you did in the daytime—and, though Mama protested, sometimes the same clothes.

During the hour of electricity in the evening, Yelena and I sat together listening to the radio, but we no longer heard Anna Akhmatova. For her survival Akhmatova, like Shostakovich, had been urged to leave Leningrad. A plane carried her away, and a spark went from the city. Still, we listened to the symphony orchestra with Olga on her violin. The poets who had stayed in the city read their latest works on the blockade. If there was no news, no readings, and no music on the radio, a metronome was set in motion so that all would know that Leningrad was still there. It was surprising how you would just sit and listen to its sound. Yelena wrote a poem about the metronome.

Silent trolley cars
silent ruined houses
a mute woman at the window
speechless with hunger
only the sound of the bombs
and the city's heartbeat

At the end of October the electricity stopped altogether: no more light, no more heat, and no more radio. To hear the radio you had to go to the loudspeakers on St. Isaac's Square. In spite of the cold, many people went, some to hear the latest news, or the music, or the sound of the metronome. Many went, as

Yelena and I often did, just for the comfort of being with others.

Though there was no heat, still everyone was praying for cold weather. Barges had been bringing food into Leningrad across Lake Ladoga, but the barges were large and cumbersome and they took nearly a day to make the trip across the lake. The Germans picked them off one by one. What the Germans did not get, the autumn storms pitched into the lake. When the lake froze, trucks would roll across the ice, trucks loaded with food. That hope kept us alive.

CHAPTER EIGHT

ALONE

November 1941

November 7, the anniversary of the Bolshevik Revolution, had always been a big holiday in the Soviet Union. Stores were closed and there were parades and dancing. This year there was no celebration. Here and there a tattered red flag was put out, but most of the stores were already closed, and no one had the strength for parades or dancing.

In our home the holiday had never been celebrated. Mama thought it should be a day of mourning. "It was the day they made the whole country a prison," she said, "and made us all prisoners."

On this November 7 Mama was quiet when she came home from the hospital. "The hunger is hard on the older people," she said. "They are so weakened, the least little cold or flu and they slip away. We have no heat in the hospital, and there is nothing to do but to pile heavy blankets on the patients, and with their thin bodies they almost smother. And Georgi, one of the doctors in the research laboratory said today that all the guinea pigs were gone."

She looked at me. We both knew where they had gone—into someone's pot. There were no cats or dogs on the streets. There was no food to give to them, and if you could find a scrap for your beloved pet to keep him alive, you did not dare to let him out onto the streets, where he would look like a banquet to some starving person.

Our apartment was always cold. There was little water for the luxury of washing. If you washed your hands, you saved the water for the next person. I felt dirty all the time. One morning I saw a woman kneeling on the ice around a well, doing her washing in freezing water.

The toilets didn't flush, and if you didn't empty the chamber pots at once, the pots froze and then you were in a pickle. And where to empty the pots? Thousands of pots were emptied on the streets, so walking was disgusting.

Every morning I had to get up and take a pail to the well at the end of the street to get our water for the day. I waited in line to get to the well, which was no more than a hole in the ice with water bubbling up. The pail seemed heavier each morning, the walk back to the apartment longer. If water was spilled on the steps, you nearly broke your neck on the ice that formed. One morning I saw an elderly woman just ahead of me with her own pail. It seemed to be too much for her, and she set it down on the sidewalk and stood there for a moment. She was so thin, there was almost no body inside the tattered clothes. I started to go up to her, thinking to carry the pail at least a little distance for her. Right there before my eyes she slipped to the ground.

People were passing by, stepping around her. "Help me," I said, for I was so weak that even her small weight was too much for me to lift. No one stopped. As I bent down over her, trying to move her away from the stream of people, I saw that she was dead. I had never seen a dead person, yet I knew. I was so frightened that some strength flowed into me, and I was able to pull her to the side of the walk.

When I looked up, someone had taken her pail and was hurrying off with it. Like the others, I went to the well and stood in line to fill my pail. I walked back to the apartment, but all the time I was thinking of the woman. I had never touched a dead person. I knew from Mama's work at the hospital that thousands were dying of starvation, but those deaths were only sad stories. Now I had touched death, and I was afraid that somehow it would cling to me and I would bring it back with me and give it to someone else. When I got home I said nothing, but I washed my hands over and over until Mama complained.

"Georgi, no one knows better than you how hard it is to get a bit of soap or a drop of water. Surely your hands are clean now."

I couldn't bring myself to tell even Mama the sad story.

In the dark mornings the ugliness and cheerlessness of the city was even more depressing. On my way to work I had to stumble along dark, filthy streets. Our brigade had finished its work in the sewers and had now joined a brigade stripping bark from all the pine and fir trees in the city parks. The bark was collected and ground up, to be added to the flour and all the other odds and ends that went into the making of our bread.

It was hard work, because the knives that were given to us were dull and we had no strength in our hands to tear at the bark. It was sad work; each time I wrenched a bit of the bark from a tree, I winced, for

I knew it meant a great old tree would die, but Dmitry said, "Better the trees than us." One afternoon I found a cocoon on one of the tree branches. I was about to toss it away when something stopped my hand. I broke off the twig to which it was fastened and put it carefully in my pocket. That evening I gave it to Yelena.

She was delighted. Her thin face broke into a smile. "Oh, Georgi, a perfect gift. I didn't think I could get through the winter, but now I have something to look forward to."

How I envied that little chrysalis, all wrapped up warmly in its cocoon with no need for food and no duty but to sleep and wait to become a butterfly. How I wished I could wrap myself up and fall asleep until the war ended. Each day it was easier and easier to lie in bed. It was such an effort to get up. I hated the thought of pushing off the blankets and coats that made a warm nest. I hated the thought of stumbling up and down the icy stairway for a pail of cold water.

I hated the thought of standing out in the cold and snow hacking away at the helpless trees.

Still, Mama found a way to lure me out of bed. "A rusk this morning, Georgi, and a half teaspoonful of jelly to sweeten your hot water. And tonight when I come home, we'll have Viktor and Olga and Yelena over to share a rusk or two. We'll act out another scene from Chekhov's *Cherry Orchard*."

All at once the day did not seem so terrible. I threw off the blankets and struggled into my coat. I had slept in my hat and gloves. As I struggled down the icy stairway and out into the cold street with the water pail, the darkness seemed punishment for summer's long days of daylight. It stayed dark now until ten o'clock in the morning, and darkness fell again by afternoon. On the streets no one looked at anyone else, afraid to see a reflection of their own miserable condition. Everyone went silently about their sad business. I saw a woman pulling her sickly husband along behind her on a sled. Another woman was carrying a small girl who must have been five or six but looked no larger than a doll. I trained myself to look straight ahead.

Rations had been cut for the third time, even for the soldiers, and everyone was so weak, work was almost impossible. Yet we had to work.

Mama came home with stories from the hospital of people brought in because of what they ate. "They are eating soap for the fat it contains and even motor oil."

One day Yelena said, "Mama told me, 'I have a special treat for you. I fried your bread in a bit of fat.'

"I asked, 'Mama, where did you get fat? And why is the bread all red?' Georgi, my mama used all that was left of her last stick of lipstick for the grease!"

Yelena had lost a third of her weight. With her thin arms and sharp collarbones she looked like a fledgling bird. We all seemed shadows of ourselves, as if someone had painted our portraits and now was painting out parts of them.

One day there was an argument between Olga and

Yelena. Yelena had called us to share a treat with them. She had come home from the library with a bag of dried beans. They had been soaking and now were bubbling on the stove. To Mama and me they were as beautiful as pearls, but Olga was slamming the pots and pans about, and Viktor had an angry look on his face.

"Yelena inherited a first edition of Pushkin's poetry from a great-great uncle," Viktor said. "Nothing could be more precious to her. This morning, without saying a word to us, she took it to the library."

"There is a book dealer who comes into the library," Olga said. "He cheated Yelena out of her most prized possession."

Tears were running down Yelena's face. "It was not like that at all," she said. "The dealer and I have become friends, and I told him about my Pushkin. He has been after me for days to sell it to him. When he promised all these beans, I couldn't resist. I was as eager to sell as he was to buy."

"We should have starved first," Olga said, but seeing Yelena's thin body and hungry pinched expression, I could not agree. When it came my turn, I said beans didn't agree with me. I was glad she had sold the book, but I couldn't eat the beans. With a sinking heart, I noticed that after Olga spoke sharply to her, Yelena could hardly get a bean down her own throat.

The next morning Dmitry and I watched a man pulling a sled with something tied to it that looked like a mummy.

"It's a body all wrapped up in a sheet and tied up like a package," Dmitry said. "My father said that if you walk by the Piskorevsky Cemetery, you can see hundreds and hundreds of such bodies, all stacked up like cords of wood because the ground is frozen and there is no place to bury them."

"Mama says just the same," I said. "There's no place to put the people who die in the hospital. They just leave them in the hospital courtyard."

The pine bark was said to contain vitamins that would help to keep people from starving. With such terrible tales to consider, that day we worked harder than ever at tearing off the bark.

We were at our lowest when I came home from work to find a package from Marya. It was battered and dented and the wrappings were loose; still, it was a miracle that it had arrived. These days the postmen were wanted elsewhere, and the mail was often not delivered. Mama opened the package and, with trembling hands, took out one unimaginable thing after another and placed them on the kitchen table. There were three chocolate bars, a large hunk of cheese, packets of dried soup, and a handful of crumbs that must have been cookies.

Hearing our shouts of joy, Olga, Viktor, and Yelena came running into the apartment.

"Are you all right?" Olga asked.

"Never better," Mama said.

They saw the glorious treats set out on the table

like so many priceless jewels. No one touched a thing. Starved as we were, we did not fall upon them and stuff them into our mouths. We just stared at them as if we were travelers who had come upon some rare sight that we ought to memorize, knowing we would never see it again.

After a few minutes Mama reached for a chocolate bar. She carefully broke off a square and divided it into five pieces, being sure that all the pieces were equal. She solemnly passed them out. I saw that our friends wanted to refuse them, but it was impossible; anyhow, we would never have allowed that. Slowly the bit of chocolate melted in our mouths. No one chewed. No one swallowed. We just sat there with that bit of chocolate on our tongues, all of us with smiles on our faces, happier than we had been for days. Then Mama carefully put it all away, first handing Olga some cheese and a packet of soup.

Olga shook her head. "No, no, that's impossible. We could not take it."

Mama got very angry. "If it had come your way, wouldn't you have shared it with us? What about the beans? Do you think we can sit here in the kitchen gorging ourselves while our dearest friends are next door starving?" Olga and Mama were both crying. They kissed, and Olga took the food. Yelena and I wet our fingers and had a battle to see who could get up the most cookie crumbs.

After the good news came bad news. The next day when I got home, I could tell Mama had been waiting for me. "Georgi, sit down. I must tell you what I have decided. There are not enough doctors and nurses at the front with the soldiers. The soldiers are giving their lives for us with no one to help and comfort them when they are injured. They are drafting nurses from the hospital. I am not sure I could say no if I wanted to. I hate to leave you, but everything must be done to help our soldiers. If they don't defeat the Germans, we will all die. I remember in the last war how much comfort the nurses were to the soldiers at the Catherine

Palace. And Georgi, when I am gone, the food that we have will go further. I wouldn't leave if I didn't feel you could manage on your own. I am so proud of you, Georgi. I don't know what I would have done without you, and Georgi, I count on you to take care of Yelena and Olga."

I didn't want Mama to go. I had told myself that I was a man and doing a man's work, but at her words I didn't feel like it; instead, I felt like a child again. I was always struggling to get Mama to realize I was grown up. Now she had, and I wasn't so happy about it.

Mama was watching me. "Georgi, I wouldn't push you out of the nest unless I was sure you could fly."

The volunteers from the hospital were leaving the next day, so Mama had little time for preparations. Olga came with a warm scarf and Yelena contributed gloves. At first Mama would not take them, but Olga said, "The hospital tents at the front will not be heated. What good will you be to the soldiers if you are sick with cold and your fingers numb?"

The morning she left, Mama put her arms around me. "It breaks my heart, Georgi, that you should have to grow up in such times."

"Mama, it was the same with you and Papa." When they were only a little older than me, Mama and Papa had faced starvation and imprisonment.

"All the more reason I didn't want it for you, Georgi, but I know you are strong. Only promise not to do anything foolish."

The apartment was empty with Marya and Mama away. Having an older sister is like having an extra mother. Now both of my mothers were gone. As sad as I was to see Mama go, still, I tried to cheer myself up by telling myself I could do as I pleased. But when there is war, you do not do as you please. I still had to tumble out of bed while it was dark and fetch a pail of water, and I still had to hurry to one of the parks where we were scraping bark.

It was dark when I returned home. Dinner was simple. I cut off a bit of bread and sliced a little of the pickled cabbage. With no money, there was no place to go; besides, you could not go out into the cold streets, for it would take you hours to warm up once you returned to your unheated home. Olga spent long hours at the radio station, playing music with the symphony. Yelena and I sat close together for warmth and read books aloud to each other. I did most of the reading, for Yelena's voice was weak. She had been thin to begin with, and when the rations were cut, the small amount of food she got and what little I could spare were hardly enough to keep her going.

"It is so strange at the library," she said. "Hundreds of people come and sit in the reading room all wrapped up in coats and mittens. They sit by our little oil lamps and read by the hour; they read as if tomorrow all the books will be gone." She sighed. "And it may happen. A German shell could easily destroy the library."

Sometimes, if she had the evening shift, Yelena spent the night at the library to avoid coming home after curfew. There were cots in one of the reading rooms for the library staff. On those nights I was shut up in my apartment with nothing to do. It was on one of those nights that I heard a scurrying noise in the cupboard. When I peeked in, a mouse darted away. Most of the Leningrad mice had long since expired of hunger. I thought, Here is a clever mouse who has not given up. I began to leave a crumb or two on the kitchen shelf. The mouse, too desperate for food to be afraid of me, would make a dash for the crumbs and then disappear. After a week the mouse was tame enough to sit and eat in front of me, but to tell the truth, I was so hungry I began to begrudge him even the crumbs. Still, I kept feeding him because when she saw him, the mouse made Yelena smile.

In the evenings I heard Yelena make her way slowly up the stairway, as if in her weakness each step were a mountain. I tried to share my food with her, but apart from a little jam or a bit of Marya's chocolate—for Yelena loved sweets—she would not take it.

"Viktor is eating at the canteen at the firehouse," she said, "so Mother and I get his bread ration." The factory where Viktor had worked had been transferred long since to Moscow from Leningrad. Now he was a volunteer fireman, working night and day to put out the fires from the constant bombing.

I was desperate to find something to do besides scrape bark, and I tried to get a job as a fireman myself, but as usual I was too young. I had nearly given up hope that I would find a proper job when I heard about the lake from Dmitry, who had heard about it from his brother.

"Vladimir is just back from Lake Ladoga. He's writing a story about it. The lake is starting to freeze. Soon the trucks will be running. He says they'll go across the lake day and night, bringing food into the city. He says it's freezing just in time, because the city is running out of flour. Soon there won't be any bread."

I began to think about the trucks on Lake Ladoga. I thought about them all the time. I saw them starting out from Leningrad, empty, driving along on the ice, and then returning loaded with flour and sugar and butter and real tea. I saw myself bringing the food to Yelena, to all the hungry people in the hospital and the people dying on the street. "Listen," I said to Dmitry, "they'll need people to unload the trucks. Why shouldn't we do it? I worked at loading and unloading the trucks from the Hermitage."

Dmitry shook his head. "I don't think the trucks have even started."

"We could go and see."

"The streetcars and buses aren't running. It must be a twenty-mile walk to the lake. We'd be icicles before we got there, and then they might not give us jobs."

I could tell he wasn't interested. What he said was

true. Still I resolved to go myself.

That evening when I told Yelena, she was against it. "Georgi, there will be men there to do the work. You'll freeze unloading the trucks in the cold and dark."

"Just because they won't let me in the army, I don't mean to spend the rest of the war stripping bark from the trees. We're all weak from hunger, and Viktor looks sicker every day. All over the city people are dying. It's important to send the trucks for the food. Unloading them will be real work."

Finally Yelena saw that I meant to go. "As for freezing," I said, "come and let me show you something."

I opened a chest and took out a box. Inside the box were the parka and boots the Samoyeds had made for Papa in Siberia. My parka and Marya's, now much too small for us, had long ago been sold. Mama wanted to keep Papa's things as a reminder of him, but I was sure she would approve.

"They look new," Yelena said. "Someone will be

sure to steal them from you."

I knew she was right and took them outside and rubbed them with dirt.

"Georgi, I wish you wouldn't take the risk."

I was almost ready to back down when later that night, while I was still sleeping, there was a loud knocking on my door. Olga burst into the room.

"Come quickly, it's Viktor."

Viktor was lying on his bed, his breathing so weak I could not be sure he was alive. There was hardly any flesh on his face, and his hands were like a skeleton's.

"He took sick at the firehouse and the men brought him home. They said he was starving." Olga was shaking with sobs.

In a whisper Yelena said, "Mama asked if he wasn't eating at the firehouse canteen, and the men said there wasn't any canteen." Two great tears slid down Yelena's cheeks. "Georgi, Viktor was just making that up so that we got his bread ration."

Olga was trying to get some hot tea between

Viktor's lips, but it only dribbled out. He took a long breath, like someone about to plunge into deep water, and he was dead.

The next hours were terrible. We wrapped Viktor in a sheet and tied it around him. As soon as it was light, I found someone with a wagon and gave him the last chocolate bar to carry Viktor to the cemetery, where there would be no burial in the frozen ground. But it was the only place I knew.

I didn't want Yelena to come. I knew what the horror looked like, but she insisted on accompanying the wagon. In a whisper she said to me, "Mama is too upset, and one of us must be there."

As we left, Yelena sighed, "If only we had flowers for Viktor, but the ground is covered with snow."

"Wait," Olga said. She choked back her tears and rummaged through a drawer, drawing out her flowered scarf and laying it over the body. We stood awkwardly by Viktor. I said a prayer. Olga took up her violin and played a bit from the Rachmaninoff violin concerto that Viktor loved and that we had often heard through the thin walls of the apartment.

The man and I carried Viktor down the stairway and laid him in the wagon. In a snowstorm Yelena and I followed the wagon to the cemetery, where the bodies were piled outside the gates, one upon the other, some not even decently wrapped. I helped the man to lay Viktor with the others. Yelena made the sign of the cross, and we turned away. Neither of us said a word. On the way back we took off our gloves and held hands, not caring about the cold, each wanting only to feel the hand of the other.

When we returned, there was no comforting Olga, for she was sure she had killed Viktor.

"He gave us his food," Olga said.

"But not only his food, Mama," Yelena told her. "He gave us his love as well. With such love we will never be hungry again."

The next day I left for Lake Ladoga.

CHAPTER NINE

"THE ROAD OF LIFE"

November 1941

I set off before light so that I would reach the lake before darkness set in. The trip through the city was one sad sight after another. Weakened by their hunger, people seemed to move in slow motion, a hopeless look on their faces. I wanted to shout at them that I was going to Lake Ladoga and that trucks laden with food would soon be moving across the ice. Just outside the city I hitched a ride part of the way with a truck carrying supplies from a Leningrad factory to the army.

"You must have a long way to go," I said.

The truck driver laughed bitterly. "I wish I did. I can't tell you where I am going, but believe me, it's not far."

So the front was close.

When I finally got to the lake's edge, it was late afternoon and already dark. There were no trucks to unload and no trucks to be seen, only a crowd of men and soldiers standing looking across a field of ice that was the lake.

"Where are the trucks?" I asked a soldier.

He laughed bitterly. "Trucks? There are no trucks. We don't know yet if the ice is safe. We have to plow a road thirty miles long across the ice. We can't do that until we are sure we have at least eight inches of ice, or the trucks will fall into the lake. They may try to get across on sleighs tomorrow. If you came for food, you might as well go home—the sleighs will never make it."

I had no intention of going home. I found a little shack crowded with soldiers and volunteers who had come to drive the trucks. I joined them and made believe

I was one of the official volunteers. A little bread was passed around and weak tea. One of the soldiers had a bottle of vodka, and that was passed around as well. Someone started a fire, and someone else was ripping boards from the floor of the shack to keep the flames going. There was a lot of excitement at the idea of testing the ice, and men were wagering rubles as to how soon the first truck would fall through the ice. At last, with the sound of snoring and the smell of unwashed bodies huddled together to keep warm, everyone fell asleep but me. I was too excited to close my eyes.

As soon as someone stirred in the morning, I sprang up and hurried to the lake. A party was getting ready to set out on the sleighs, but they were short some men. There were loud complaints that the volunteers were sleeping off their vodka. Before I thought of what I was doing, I stepped forward. A man called Sasha motioned to me to join him on his sleigh. He was in his thirties, short and stocky like a tree trunk and with a loud voice and a loud laugh. He said,

"Young friend, come up here and keep me company. You are a cheerful soul, not like these long-faced types who grumble about this and that. You won't complain if these sad, bony horses fall over halfway there."

Pleased to be chosen, I climbed up eagerly onto his sleigh. "They say there will be oats and hay in Kobona," I told him.

"That's what I like to hear. Good news. Always look on the sunny side." He leaned forward and began to talk to the horses.

"Let me tell you, fellows, what you two horses are doing is a great thing. Today you are heroes of the Soviet Union. Stalin himself will pin a medal on your harnesses. Never mind the cold and ice, just say to yourselves you are out on a run for pleasure, galloping across the lake for a lark. That's the way. Keep going, and on the other side you will have all the oats and hay you can eat."

We set out slowly, the men in the lead sleigh stopping to measure the ice, which was only six inches. It might support us, but not a truck. When we reached the open lake, the wind blew so hard, we had to clutch each other to keep from being blown away. The leader in the first sleigh would call out, "Thin ice," and the call would be passed back. We would then have to go to the left or the right to find stronger ice.

I thanked the Samoyeds a million times for their gift. I was hungry and weak, but their parka and boots kept me warm. I thought of my Samoyed friend, the shaman, and how he would walk ahead of his people, pointing out the safest and quickest route. I wished he were guiding us across the lake.

It was late afternoon when we came to open water. Some of the men cursed, sure that after all our efforts we would have to turn back. One of the men climbed out of his sleigh and walked to one side until we heard him call from a distance that he was on solid ice again. We followed him and kept going. Once we stopped for a short time, and Sasha shared a bit of bread with me.

At times the wind blowing across the lake was so

strong, the sleigh was blown off its course. We came to a wide crack in the ice. Sasha cursed in a string of words I had never heard before. Along with the other sleighs, we headed south and then east again to avoid the crack. Hours later we reached the island of Zelenets, where we were ordered to rest the horses, whose warm bodies were sending up ghosts of white steam into the freezing air. We were given great hunks of bread and real tea with sugar cubes to drink with it. But there were no oats or hay for our poor horses. Sasha looked at me. Together we looked at our starving, shivering horses. We fed the horses half our bread and smiled at each other as the horses slobbered up the sugar cubes we held out to them.

We were back on the ice again. It was midnight before we reached Kobona, on the other side of the lake. A crowd had waited up for us, and we heard their cheers as we pulled the sleighs onto land. There was food there, real bread with butter and real tea. I put half the buttered bread in my pocket for Yelena and even wrapped the used tea leaves in my handkerchief to save.

There was no time to rest. The sleighs were loaded with cereal, cottonseed cakes, and sugar, but again there was no food for the horses. How were the poor beasts to pull loaded sleighs back the thirty miles across the ice? Yet the food on the sleighs would save many lives. I remembered how the Samoyeds told of the reindeer digging with their hooves to get at the moss that lay under the snow's covering. I told this to Sasha, who clapped me roughly on the back and said, "You see, I knew from the first you would bring me luck." Together we swept away snow and pulled up the dried grass, which the horses eagerly munched. When the others saw what we were about, they did the same.

The loaded sleighs began their return trip across the ice, and the next morning we brought the first load of food into Leningrad.

We unloaded the sleighs onto trucks and climbed

onto the trucks ourselves. Once the trucks reached the warehouses, we unloaded them again. We all had been dreaming of taking a bit of food for our efforts, but that dream soon ended. As we were unloading, we heard a shot and saw one of the drivers fall to the ground. A soldier put his gun back into his holster. "There are plenty of bullets," he said, "for the next man who tries to steal food."

Near the end of November the ice was thick enough for the trucks. Sasha was chosen to be a driver. I begged to go along to help with the loading and unloading. "If your truck breaks down, I know all about engines," I said.

Sasha agreed. "You are only a boy, but you are strong and good-natured and you don't argue with me. If you know something about trucks, so much the better."

I expected the trucks to be empty crossing the lake, but half of the city wanted to escape. The authorities agreed. The more people left the city, the more food there would be for those who remained, but there was only so much room in the trucks. Unless they had the proper papers, people were turned away, so the place from which the trucks set off was crowded with pushing, hysterical people offering money and jewelry and gold to get on one of them. If a passenger was taken on without the proper papers, the truck driver was severely punished.

"They shoot us," Sasha said.

The refugees were punished as well, for the trip in the bed of a truck across the lake with the cold and the wind was a fearful ordeal. Some did not make it.

On our return the trucks took their loads of food to the warehouses in the freight yards; from there it was distributed across the city. Once a week I would get a day off, and after unloading the truck, I would make my way across the city to our apartment. In Kobona I could sometimes get a little extra butter or cereal, so Olga looked more cheerful and Yelena began to have a little color to her face.

Yelena had worked out a scheme with the library that pleased her. "I worried about all the people not strong enough to come to the library. How terrible I should feel if I didn't have a book close by. Even on the coldest day and no matter how hungry I am, a favorite book will give me a minute or two of peace. They are allowing me to take books to the hospitals, and oh, Georgi, if you could see the faces of some of the patients when I put a book in their hands—it is nearly as good as bread."

At the end of November the weather turned warm. People breathed a sigh of relief, thinking they would be saved from freezing to death, but on the lake it was a disaster. The ice began to thaw. One day on the way back we came to a soft spot. Sasha did not pause but gunned the engine, and we roared across, almost flying over the ice. When I looked behind me, I saw the truck that had tried to follow us sink into the water and disappear. I covered my eyes with my hands and groaned.

"*Nichevo*, never mind," Sasha said, as he said to everything.

"We have to go back," I shouted. I was shaking at our narrow escape and horrified at what I had seen.

Sasha said, "We would fall through ourselves. Besides, the food we are carrying will save a thousand lives."

I knew he was right, but it was terrible to me that people were dying in the city from hunger and dying on the lake to end the hunger.

CHAPTER TEN

RETURN

December 1941

We had our first good news from the front. The town of Tikhvin had been recaptured from the Germans, and our soldiers had retaken the railroad as far as the crucial Mga station. Along with all the food our trucks were bringing into the city, small amounts of food were also beginning to arrive by train.

The temperature the day before Christmas was below zero with a heavy snow. There was no electricity and so no radio for an official announcement; nevertheless, the word spread from house to house and person to person. Rations were going to be increased. It did not matter that the increase was only a very little—the movement for the first time was upward. People in the streets were slapping one another on the backs, tears were flowing.

At the bakery the women behind the counters, who were usually sullen and unhappy over having to say the word no all the time, were now smiling. It was only a little more, but what a Christmas surprise!

The people of Kobona provided tea and food, bread with butter, and farm cheese as a Christmas treat for the truck drivers. I kept a knapsack with me, and into the knapsack went most of my food. In the freezing cold everything would keep. Sasha saw what I was doing and scolded me. "You need your strength to heave those boxes and barrels in and out of the truck."

On Christmas morning I prepared a feast of real tea with sugar, thick slices of bread—dried but, still, with the taste of butter on them, and slices of cheese. Olga and Yelena were speechless.

At last Olga said, "Where have you stolen the

food from? Let's hurry and eat the evidence before we are all dragged off to prison."

Yelena said, "It's a dream. If we touch it, it will disappear."

The government discouraged the celebration of Christmas. But Yelena was in great spirits after our feast. Laughing, she let a candle drop its melting wax over a bowl of water. It was an old superstition that a girl would find some sign of her future husband if at Christmas she dropped wax into water.

"Let's see what we have." She stared at the puddle of wax. "It looks like four wheels. Why, it's a truck!" She smiled. "Who can that be?"

Olga got into the spirit of the day, and taking up her violin, she played while Yelena and I sang Christmas hymns. It was the first time I had seen her smile since Viktor's death. That night we wished one another *S Rozhdestvom Khristovom*, Merry Christmas, and went off to our beds with, miracle of miracles, full stomachs. If only Mama and Marya had been there, I thought, the day would have been perfect.

On Lake Ladoga the Germans never stopped shelling our trucks or dropping bombs on us, so the only time it was safe to be on the ice was at night, which was when we made most of our runs. The trucks had begun to break down. I would tell Sasha what was needed, and he would scrounge parts from old trucks in the city that could no longer run because there was no gasoline for anything but authorized vehicles. I would replace the worn parts and hold my breath while Sasha turned on the ignition.

The German shelling increased. Signs went up along the prospekt that read: THE SUNNY SIDE OF THE STREET IS THE DANGEROUS SIDE. That was where most of the bombs fell. While the shelling went on, we all walked on the less dangerous side.

The weather on the ice road was below zero, then ten, twenty, and one night forty degrees below zero. Still we drove on. Men were sent to establish posts every mile along the ice road to control the traffic and see to the trucks that broke down. All along the route there were antiaircraft batteries fighting off the German planes that tried to pick off our trucks. There were only a few hours of light now, and the whole world seemed wrapped in darkness, but the darkness protected our trucks.

The number of people escaping from Leningrad was increasing every day. It was said several hundred thousand had left the city. We were offered every kind of bribe—rubles, gold, vodka—to take passengers who had no proper papers. Many of the drivers took the bribes, but Sasha would not. "What good would the gold and vodka do me in the grave?" he said. The penalty was immediate execution, no questions asked.

Very few tried to return to the city. Who would want to come into poor starving Leningrad? It was the last day of the year when I saw a woman climb onto the load of supplies in the truck ahead of us and find a protected spot for herself in the back. She was wrapped in a heavy coat, and her face was hidden by a cap pulled almost over her eyes. The rest of her face was covered to her nose with a scarf, but I had seen her covered in the same way a hundred times in Siberia, and I recognized the coat. It was Marya. I rushed toward the truck, but the truck took off and my cries were lost in the wind.

Sasha yelled, "Are you coming or do I go without you?"

"Sasha," I pleaded, climbing up beside him. "Can you catch up with that truck? My sister is in it!"

"Your sister! How can she be so stupid? Only a fool would come back to a dying city."

"Hurry. I don't want to lose sight of her."

"Is she pretty?"

"Never mind. She has a boyfriend who is a soldier and bigger than you."

"Why should I hurry and risk the truck breaking down if I don't have a chance?" Still, always happy for a challenge, he raced along as fast as the old truck could manage.

Across the ice we went, my eyes never off Marya and Marya with no idea I knew she was there.

The ice road was secure now, with several feet of ice, and we made the trip in the usual four hours. I jumped out of our truck and began running. All the while Sasha was calling after me, "Hey. We have to unload. Come back."

Before she knew what was happening, I was lifting Marya from her truck.

"Georgi! It's a miracle. Where did you come from?"

We both were so stuffed with coats and mittens that we could hardly get our arms around each other.

"What are you doing back here?" I demanded.

"I had to come back. The treasures from the museum are all safely tucked away underground. There was nothing more to be done. Every time I put a bit of bread in my mouth, I could not swallow it for thinking of how hungry you and Mama must be, and

I've heard nothing from Andrei. I had to come back. Georgi, what are you doing here?"

Sasha was shouting to me. "Listen, Marya," I said. "Come with me to the warehouse. I have to unload our truck. Then we'll go home and I'll tell you everything."

We had had no way of writing to Marya, so there was much to tell. Mama was at an army hospital and Andrei was still somewhere at the front, I told her on the way home.

"Mama gone! I can't believe it. Oh, Georgi, what a sad homecoming."

For Marya the walk through the city was terrible. She was seeing the ruined Leningrad for the first time. "Why is that man selling dirt?" She was horrified.

"It isn't exactly dirt. When the warehouses burned, the sugar burned as well. It melted into the earth. They have dug up the earth with its bit of sugar."

The Gostiny Dvor, the market where we had loved to shop as children, had been bombed and was now only a blackened shell. Hundreds of starving people stood in lines at the stores, waiting for their rations. There were women dragging sleds with grown men too weak to walk. We passed the cemetery with its stacks of bodies that could not be buried in the frozen ground, and I had to tell Marya how we had taken Viktor there. Crater holes from the German shelling were everywhere, stores were boarded up, the trolley cars stood like silent ghosts. Everything was dark and blacked out, as if the city were not there at all.

"Mama used to say our city was safe as long as the angel still stands on the column in Palace Square, but how can our poor city survive this?" Marya began to cry; in the cold the tears froze on her cheeks as if all the warmth had gone out of the world.

When at last we were seated in our apartment with Olga and Yelena, drinking the real tea Marya had brought, Marya was more cheerful. "I'm glad I came back. Things are sure to get better—they can't be worse."

Yelena said, "I hope so, but things at the library are certainly getting worse. The ink is frozen in the inkwells. All the pencils have been burned for fuel in peoples' *burzhuika*s. What is even worse, more and more books are being stolen to burn for fuel. I can't blame people, but they are carrying off some of my favorites. Yesterday I saw a man put a book under his coat, and I was sure it was our last copy of Lermontov's poems. Before I could stop myself, I ran up to him with a copy of *The Collected Works of Stalin* and said to him, 'Surely this will make better reading for you,' and I snatched away the poems, saying nothing about the theft. He seemed satisfied, since the *Works* was much fatter than the poems. Now I am putting out government books and hiding the poets."

The next day Marya hurried to the Hermitage to see her old friends and came back with her own sad story.

"Georgi! There are hundreds and hundreds of

people living in the museum. They are down in the cellars in the bomb shelters. Their own homes have been destroyed by German shells. They are commandeering all the building material Comrade Orbeli ordered so that he could restore the damaged museum when the war is over. And what are they commandeering it for? For coffins, Georgi!"

That evening Yelena, Olga, Marya, and I, along with all those who were strong enough to be out in the cold, went to St. Isaac's Square to listen to the news over the loudspeakers, followed by poets reading their poems. When Marya heard the poet Simonov's poem "Wait for Me," with its sad words, "Wait for me, and I'll return, wait for me in snow, wait for me in rain, only please wait," cold tears once again ran down her cheeks, and I knew she was thinking of Andrei.

CHAPTER ELEVEN

FYODOR

February 1942

Typhus had broken out in the city. I urged Yelena to stay at home.

"What! Leave the library and let people come in and take all my favorite books?"

It was not only the typhus that was making the city dangerous. It was a murderous city. Desperate people were willing to do whatever was necessary to stay alive. People stole and murdered for food or ration cards. Now that a ration card could not be replaced, a stolen card spelled your doom.

Dmitry and I were walking down the prospekt

when we saw a man push an old woman down and steal her purse. Though we hardly had the strength to walk, we found ourselves running after the man. Dmitry tackled him and I sat on top of him. We found the ration card.

"Don't turn me in. They will shoot me. Look, look, I have three little ones and they are starving. My wife died yesterday." He held out a crumpled photograph of three children gathered around a smiling woman. It was true: If we turned him in, he would be shot, and then his three children would surely die.

"But what about the old woman you shoved to the ground and left helpless with no card?" I demanded.

He only sobbed. Dmitry and I looked at each other. We let the man go and returned her card to the old woman. She blessed us, tears running down her cheeks. Dmitry and I walked on. We had no heart for anything. We no longer recognized our city.

It was on that day that Marya brought home a child. He looked to be about four years old, dressed in rags, his legs like matchsticks, great hollows under his eyes, his arms and hands all blue veins.

Marya carried him into the apartment. He was so weak, he could not stand up but slumped to the floor. She laid him on the sofa and hurried to make him a bit of kasha from the small hoard of cereal that she had brought back from Sverdlovsk.

"Marya," I demanded, "why have you brought this child here? We said we wouldn't touch the cereal until the last moment." I could not see what the child had to do with us.

"The child is dying of starvation, Georgi. His parents were staying at the Hermitage. They are dead, his father last week, his mother today. She begged me to take care of him. His name is Fyodor. The father worked as a guard at the Hermitage. There is no one else to care for the boy. The children's homes are overflowing. They have no food and they are full of sickness. Between Olga and Yelena and us, we can care for him. I feel so helpless—this at least will be one thing I can do."

I reached out to pat Fyodor on the head in a friendly manner, and he shrank from me as if I were going to hit him.

"Hey, fellow," I said, "I just want to be friends."

Fyodor had eyes only for the cupboard from which Marya had taken the bit of cereal.

Marya said, "It's not his fault, Georgi. Things are very bad at the Hermitage; it's dog-eat-dog. You must be patient with Fyodor."

I thought he might be more friendly after he ate, but no, he curled up under the table and would not come out.

Yelena came and tried to lure him out with a story. Olga sang him a song. But nothing would make him say a word to us or make him come out from under the table.

It must have been two or three in the morning when I heard the faintest noise. I was on one cot and Fyodor in his nest under the table in a bed Marya had made up for him, or so I thought. In the dark room I saw a shadow creeping toward the cupboard. I reached out to grasp Fyodor's arm and felt his teeth sink into my hand, which luckily was enclosed in mittens. Hearing my yelp, Marya sprang out of bed, and the two of us pursued the boy, who now was back under the table, rolled into as small a ball as possible.

"Look," I said, sticking my head under the table, "we know you are hungry, but we are giving you extra food. If you steal what we have, we will all die of starvation, and then where will you be?"

He growled like a dog whose bone has been threatened. Marya made the cupboard fast with a tangle of string, and we all went back to sleep. In the morning the child was calm enough to let Marya wipe his face and hands with a little snow and give him some pine-needle extract that was handed out to keep us from scurvy, since there were no fruits or vegetables in all the city.

We couldn't tidy up Fyodor nor wash his clothes,

for there was no extra water. Every ounce had to be extracted from the icy well, then carried through the streets and up the icy steps. Grimy as he was, he went off with Marya to the Hermitage for the day and I hurried off to Ladoga for my week of trucking. By the end of the week, when I returned, Fyodor gave me a shy smile, and when I held out a lump of sugar I had brought from Kobona, he climbed upon my lap. It seemed a kind of miracle that one person had been saved and would live.

There was more good news. Marya showed me a letter from Mama.

February 23, 1942

My dearest Marya and Georgi,
Your letter was forwarded to me from the hospital. Thank the Lord that Marya is safe and back in Leningrad. I am so happy that the two of you are once again together. I am

writing to Olga and Yelena. Such sad news
you sent about Viktor. He was a good man,
and only a pessimist because he was so good
himself, it was sad for him to see that others
could not live up to his high expectations.

I cannot tell you where I am, except to
say that I am close to the front and that all
day long soldiers are brought in to us. We do
all that we can, but often it is not enough.
There are days when I want to pick up a gun
and go out to fight the enemy myself.

I have saved the good news for the end.
Last week a soldier came in with a bad leg
wound, but we have a fine doctor here and
after an operation the leg is doing well. I
was the one who assisted at the operation.
And who is the soldier? It is Andrei. He
is alive and well and is shortly to be sent
back to Leningrad to work at General Staff
headquarters, for it will be a long time before

he can fight again. I am enclosing a letter he
has written to Marya.

> *God bless you both,*
> *Mama*

Marya danced me around the room, laughing and crying, while little Fyodor looked on with wide eyes.

"When are you going to show me Andrei's letter?" I asked.

"Never. I don't want any of your teasing."

The following week when I got home, Andrei was there. At least I thought that was who it was, but he looked very unlike Andrei. The stranger supported himself with a walking stick, and he was as thin as the stick. His head was shaved, and the well-groomed look and proper uniform had given way to the stubble of a beard and a uniform put together from bits and pieces that were either too large or too small. What was even more puzzling was Andrei's manner. There was none of his easy friendliness. I noticed a puzzled look on Marya's face.

After we welcomed each other, Andrei said, "So, Georgi, Marya tells me you are traveling across Ladoga's Road of Life. I'm impressed."

"They should have let me into the army," I said. "I could have fought as well as the next one."

"I don't doubt that, Georgi, but to tell you the truth, you are doing more good bringing food into the city. Anyone can walk backward."

"Backward? Surely the army has won a few battles."

"Not many. How could they? The soldiers have no weapons, and the artillery is always someplace else. We are sacrificing our lives because we don't have the means to fight. They were none too happy to see me at General Staff headquarters. They don't want to hear my sad stories."

Marya quickly said, "Andrei, watch what you say. You know what happens to anyone who speaks out."

"I'm not telling them anything they don't know."

"What they know and what they want to hear are two different things, Andrei."

All the time we were talking, Fyodor was peeking at Andrei from under the table, where he had retreated at the sight of an unknown person, and one in a uniform.

Andrei bent down. "Come here, young man, and see what I have for you."

Fyodor poked his head out a bit, and Andrei offered him a piece of toffee wrapped in silver foil. "They were good to us in the hospital," he said.

Fyodor grabbed at the candy and burrowed under the table again.

"Fyodor, shame on you," Marya said. "Thank Andrei politely."

Instead Fyodor spat out the candy and began to cry. Marya got on her knees to see what the trouble was. "Oh, Fyodor, I never thought." She held up the piece of toffee, which now had a tooth in it. "All the children's teeth are loose from their diet. Come and I'll give you a little warm tea with a bit of jam." At this Fyodor emerged, brushing away his tears.

In a bitter voice Andrei said, "See what has become of our little ones. The war has robbed them of their childhood, all those years when they should be happy and carefree. Their lives are ruined."

"You have become like a bear with a sore head, Andrei," I said. "You are a pessimist. Look at what happened to my mother when she was little—her dearest friends executed. Look at Marya and me, our parents snatched away in the middle of the night, Papa dead, and still there have been happy days for all of us. The war can't last forever."

"And you are too much of an optimist, Georgi. Being a little hungry here in Leningrad or driving trucks across the lake is not like a battlefield."

That was too much. In an angry voice I said, "You should have been here to see Viktor die because he wanted to keep Olga and Yelena from starving. You should have seen the trucks that went through the ice with the drivers going down into the icy water! I have seen bad things as well as you have."

"I didn't mean to attack you, Georgi. Marya has told me how you have risked your life on the lake. Olga said they would never have survived without your help." Andrei hid his face in his hands. "Forgive me. I'm not myself."

Fyodor, who clutched his glass of tea with both hands, looked at Andrei. He took a quick sip and then held out the glass to Andrei. "Don't cry," he said. "You can have some of my tea."

Andrei looked at him. For the first time, a smile spread over his face. "No, thank you, Fyodor, but come and sit beside me." Andrei turned to me. "You are right to be an optimist. If a hungry child can share his food, anything is possible."

I think at General Staff headquarters they did not want to hear what he had to say and were glad to be rid of him, so Andrei was often at our house. As soon as Fyodor heard the tap of Andrei's walking stick on the stairway, he ran to the door. Andrei would lay down his stick and swing Fyodor about until the boy was breathless with laughter. Andrei and Fyodor knew that they had both come to the edge of a cliff and, by holding on to each other, had stopped just short of tumbling off.

CHAPTER TWELVE

SPRING THAW

March 1942

Every place we went, cold and hunger were there. We bundled up in our coats and mittens, inside as well as outside. When a sweater or a mitten wore out, Marya would unravel and reknit it. When we sat together in the apartment, our words came out in little white puffs. We stayed near one another, not just Yelena with me and Andrei with Marya, but all of us, sitting close beside the others, keeping away any little drafts we could, sharing a bit of the other people's warmth. At night Marya, Fyodor, Olga, and Yelena slept all together in a little heap like a basket full of puppies.

When I wasn't on the lake, I joined them.

Our closeness was for the warmth but also for the company. As deaths in the city increased, we were afraid to let one another out of our sight. We pretended there had been no change in our appearance. We stayed away from mirrors, not wanting to see our sallow faces, hollowed cheeks, mangy hair, cracked lips, and rheumy eyes. Marya no longer had the strength to walk to the Hermitage. She stayed home all day with Fyodor.

Together Andrei and Marya would try to make Fyodor forget his hunger with stories and games, and in the trying for a few minutes they would forget their own hunger. Marya told him stories of our travels with the Samoyeds through the woods and how we had had our own reindeer to ride. Andrei made little soldiers from bits of wood and set up battles. Fyodor loved to move the soldiers about and knock down all the German soldiers. As long as they could keep him amused, Fyodor would forget about his empty belly.

The jam and cabbage and the winter vegetables had long been used up. Even the dried rusks were gone. We would use the same meatless bone over and over again with a potato to make soup. Andrei ate at the army canteen, and each day he would come with some bit of food he had saved from his meal: a nugget of bread spread with a teaspoon of lard, a slippery piece of cooked onion to toss into the pot for flavor and nourishment, and, one glorious day, a half slice of bacon. I knew what a sacrifice he was making, for Dmitry's brother Vladimir had told him that the soldiers were so hungry at General Staff headquarters that there were fights over a crumb of bread that fell to the floor.

Yelena was bringing home books. We would carefully take them apart to get at the paste that held the books together, for the paste was made with flour. When all the paste had been scraped into the soup bowl, we burned the books in our little stove. Each book we burned brought tears to Yelena's eyes. She tried to pick out books that meant little, such as a report from some bureaucratic committee on the gross product of the steel industry, but still it was a book and she cried.

I no longer had a job. The number of trucks had been cut down because the ice on Lake Ladoga was breaking up. With nothing to do, I stayed around the house, getting on Marya's nerves. I got on Andrei's nerves as well, with my daily complaints at not being able to join the army. I had heard they were taking seventeen-year-olds now, and I kept asking, "If seventeen, why not sixteen? I'll be sixteen in September."

"Georgi, you don't know what you are saying. First of all they are not taking sixteen-year-olds, and secondly if you could hear the reports of the battles and see the number of dead and injured, if you could hear the pleas of the generals for more guns and ammunition so they could at least defend themselves, you wouldn't be talking about joining the army."

"All you are doing is showing me how much I am needed and giving me more reason to join."

"If what I say makes you eager to join the army, you are a fool, Georgi."

"I've heard you say you are going back when your leg is healed."

"That is another matter entirely," Andrei said.

"If you can go, why can't I?" And so it went. With empty stomachs and freezing hands, we were all irritable. March still seemed like the middle of winter—and then a miracle happened.

The weather warmed. One day there was snow on the ground, and the next day the snow had turned into puddles. We heard dripping as the icicles that hung from the roof melted in the spring sun.

Andrei burst into the apartment to announce, "The towns along the railroad have been freed. More food is sure to come by the railroad." By the end of the week rations were increased. You did not have to get up at four in the morning and get in line to get your ration of bread. If you were in line by six, the bread would be there.

It was possible to walk about without freezing. The city was still being shelled, and you never knew when your building might be hit; even a walk down the block was dangerous. Still, Dmitry and I walked bravely about, enjoying the sun and the unaccustomed warmth and trying not to notice all the bombed-out houses missing walls and roofs.

The public baths had been closed for lack of water and heat, but now a few of them opened. For the first time you could get clean. There was less water in the baths than usual and the water was none too pure, but washing away the grime was heaven. Dmitry and I thrashed about in the water, splashing each other like seals until the manager of the bath threatened to throw us out. Marya and Yelena went off to wash their hair for the first time in weeks and came home skipping up the stairway.

But the city itself was foul and filthy with dirt. People who hadn't the strength to take their dead to the cemetery had left them on the sidewalks. The only thing missing was garbage, for there was none. Every bit of peel and every bone was eaten or gnawed.

Notices began to appear all over the city declaring March 15 as Cleanup Day. There were announcements over the loudspeakers at St. Isaac's Square. Posters were everywhere. Even those weak with hunger looked forward to the day.

More than two hundred thousand people turned out. They poured from bombed-out houses that had looked as if they were empty. They crept out of hovels and alleyways and the shelter of boxes. We were all shabby and bedraggled. If any one of us had stood still, we surely would have been scooped up as a bit of rubbish.

Dmitry and I came with shovels, Olga and Yelena with brooms. Andrei had made Fyodor a toy shovel. You could not imagine such a sight. People who looked as if they could not move a matchstick were scraping mounds of dirt from the streets and sidewalks. For months strangers, full of fear and despair, had not spoken to one another on the street. Now we called to one another, laughing cheerfully at our ugly, gruesome tasks. Trucks were deployed to pick up dirt and carry it from the city. Trucks also came for the dead. Our little party chose the Summer Garden, heading for the spot where we had had our picnic in June. How different it was. The trees were gone, scraped for bark and then cut altogether for firewood. The last tatters of snow lay like dirty gray rags on the lawn. Refuse was everywhere. We set ourselves a small task.

"We'll clear the space where we held our picnic," Olga said. With a great sigh at its weight, I lifted my shovel. Once we started, there was no stopping us. We could not guess where our strength was coming from, but when we had finished, there was a little patch of the Summer Garden as it used to be. All around us other workers were clearing their own spaces. It was late afternoon when we finished. We were too tired to walk home and cheerfully sat there on the warm March day. Olga had her eyes closed, her face raised to the sun. Fyodor leaned against Marya, who was telling him that one day she would bring him to the garden and he could play in the fountain and they would have a picnic and all the *piroshki* he wanted to eat. Fyodor's eyes were very wide at this fairy tale.

"The blockade must come to an end soon," Yelena said.

Dmitry and I looked at each other. I shook my head at him. I did not want to take Yelena's hope from her, for hope was as nourishing as food, but Dmitry's brother had been home from the front and reported to Dmitry that the soldiers were as weak and hungry as we were.

"At least," I said, "summer is coming and there will be daylight and warmth."

From the subdued tone of my voice Yelena understood what I was thinking. "Yes," she said, "and we will have the grass to eat."

It was only the next evening that Olga pounded on our door. When I opened it, Olga and Yelena burst into the room. Olga was holding a sheaf of papers in her hand and waving it in the air like a banner.

"You needn't knock me down," I said. "What do you have in your hand? The German surrender?"

"Just as good," Olga said. "It's the score for Shostakovich's Leningrad Symphony. You must promise not to tell a soul."

Marya and I looked at each other in amazement. There had been rumors that Shostakovich had finished the symphony, but it was something else to see it in Olga's hands. We nodded our heads.

"The orchestra is going to perform the symphony. It's an extraordinary piece of work, and Shostakovich has dedicated it to the city of Leningrad. Our orchestra will play it this spring. They even sent the manuscript from Moscow in a plane."

"It was just a little plane," Yelena said, "and the pilot risked his life flying over the German troops."

"Our director, Eliasberg, says it is a masterpiece. The problem is we don't have enough copies of the violin parts. We need more. Yelena and I want you to help us."

"Olga," Marya said, "Georgi and I know nothing about music."

"We will teach you. All you have to do is copy it onto this music paper they sent. You just go one note at a time, but you must copy it exactly or there will be chaos."

We sat down at the kitchen table and note by note, hour by hour, we worked until one in the morning. The spring warmth had not yet crept into the apartment. We tried to copy with our gloves on, which was impossible, so we cut the fingers off the gloves. The four of us worked away until we had all the copies completed. Although I couldn't read a note of the music, I was sure the composer was much better with his pen than with his shovel.

Gathering up the pages, Olga promised, "For all your work, I'll see that you have the best seats in the house when we give the concert."

The next week the streetcars began to run along the prospekt. It was only a small thing; still, the trolleys had been such a part of the prospekt that it was like sleeping giants coming to life. You had the feeling that you could go somewhere even if there was no place to go.

The city was smaller now. With all the evacuations and all the deaths, it was only a third of the size it had once been. The new emptiness was frightening, but the food stretched a little more. The ice was floating out of the river—no more struggling to a well with the pail and walking up the icy steps. Now that I could dip my pail into a canal or the river, one more misery had disappeared with the ice.

The thought of a fish cooking on the stove had occurred to everyone, and the banks of the Neva were crowded with fishermen, including me. If it hadn't been for the desperately eager look on the faces of the fishermen, it might have been any holiday. First there was the question of what to use for bait. I had stopped by the Summer Garden and dug several worms. For

just a moment I wondered how they would taste, perhaps cooked in a broth.

I joined some other fishermen at the Moika Canal.
My heart was racing as the hook descended into the
water. Would I be lucky? At the end of the crowded
row, a man pulled in a large codfish. Everyone took
heart and waited expectantly. Unhappily, few fish
were biting. Why weren't they as hungry as we were?
The lucky man with the fish was cutting off a hunk of
flesh in exchange for a measure of flour. I thought of
the times I had fished in Siberia, first with Marya and
then with the Samoyeds, when we had nearly met a
terrible fate for fishing in the territory of their shaman.

Overhead the gulls were screeching, wanting their
share. One hour followed another with only a few dis-
appointing pulls at the hook as a clever fish grabbed a
bit of worm and went his way. At last I felt a pull on
the line and I yanked. There was an ugly-looking
sucker, a bottom-feeder and scavenger that no one in
good times would have eaten, yet I called out, "Look

at this beauty" and hurried home with the ugly beast, as pleased as I would have been with a bowl of caviar.

What rejoicing there was. Marya took the creature out to the balcony and scraped away at its scales and pulled out all the innards, to the delight of Fyodor, who wanted to hear the story of each slimy bit.

"He is sure to grow up a great scientist," Marya said, trying to decide whether any of the insides should go into the soup.

That night we had a party with Yelena and Olga. Yelena made up a poem for Fyodor about the fish.

Trading water for air
you leap into our pot.
We are sorry to eat you
but thanks a lot.

There was not much time for fishing, for Dmitry and I were assigned a new job, a strange one. The shelling and the bombing had not stopped. Day and night the German planes flew over us, and from the edge of the city their mortars fired away. The German spring offensive was under way, and once again the Germans were trying to take Leningrad. Half the buildings in the city had been shelled, and many were destroyed.

The shelled and boarded buildings were depressing people, so it was decided that something must be done. They ordered false fronts put up. Dmitry and I and our brigade were given sheets of plywood and paint. We made a mock-up of the front of a building as it had appeared before the bombing, and then we painted on windows and doors. The false fronts that covered the burned-out buildings might have been a scene for a stage play. There was a lot of competition to see who could make the most realistic building. I painted a little dog on the false front of the house I was making. It was the only dog in the city, and it made the people who passed by smile. Dmitry, who was clever with paints, did me one better. In one of the windows he painted a scene of a feast, a dining-room table laden with a great roast, heaps of potatoes, a green salad, and a big chocolate cake. There was standing room only by his painting.

The amazing thing was that when we were given the photographs to copy showing how the houses had once looked, we saw that the pictures had been taken by our "German spy," Josif Vasilyevich Vronsky.

CHAPTER THIRTEEN

THE LENINGRAD SYMPHONY

Spring, summer 1942

We began to hear unfamiliar sounds coming through the walls: Olga was practicing music so strange and powerful that when you heard it, you just stopped what you were doing and listened. We knew she must be practicing the Shostakovich. The music would go on for several bars and then die down as if a phonograph needed winding. The first chance I had, I asked, "Olga, how is it going?" She began to cry.

"Why are you crying?"

"It is so hard to play. My arms don't have the strength do the work justice. I can practice for only a short time. It's that way for all the musicians. We don't think we can do it. The first day, Conductor Eliasberg could hardly move his arms to direct us. The rehearsal was to go on all afternoon, and after just a quarter of an hour we had to stop. Ivan had only enough wind to make a squeak with his French horn." Her voice changed to a whisper, as if she could not say the words aloud. "Saddest of all, Georgi, out of a hundred musicians, only fifteen of us are left. The others have died of starvation or been killed by the bombs. Where can we find musicians to take their places?"

I tried to cheer her. "Your strength will come back," I promised. Each day the music on the other side of the wall did become a little stronger and went on a little longer.

The orchestra found its replacements. Andrei said, "Yes, we know all about the symphony. We sent out a notice from General Staff headquarters that any soldier who played an instrument was to report at once for duty here in the city, and good news—

they've discovered a military band at the front, sent there to cheer the soldiers. They are on their way."

While Olga practiced every day, Dmitry and I, like most of the city, had become farmers. By order of the authorities, rows of cabbages, potatoes, and turnips were planted in all the parks and guarded by policemen as if the vegetables that sprang up were made of gold.

Dmitry and I dug and planted day after day, breaking up the soil and bending over to plant seeds and potatoes. When I came home at night, I could barely get up the stairs. The gardens we were planting in the parks were the property of the city, but here and there were small private gardens, and along the streets wherever a weed sprang, someone immediately pounced on it. I myself brought home a dandelion I had found growing through a crack in the sidewalk. It went right into the soup, flower and all.

"What questions I am getting at the library, Georgi," Yelena said. "'How can I make a soup from clover?' 'How can I gather the nettles to cook without stinging my hands?'"

It had been so long since people had seen something green on their tables, there was not a patch of lawn left in the city. As soon as something green appeared, it was eaten. Yelena had been right in her prediction that we would eat grass.

The city was handing out vegetable seeds, but where to plant them? Anything grown in an untended plot could be stolen. I was standing on our balcony when the idea came to me. An hour later I arrived home carrying a heavy burlap bag.

Marya stared at it. "Georgi, what do you have?"

I dragged the heavy bag out onto the balcony and emptied the soil onto the balcony floor. "Georgi!" Marya shrieked. "What are you doing to our balcony?"

I laughed. "Calm yourself, Marya. We are going to have our own garden this summer. Our peas and beans and lettuce will be better than rubies and emeralds. No more standing in line for a few shriveled potatoes that cost a fortune. Now, quickly, get Olga and Yelena and tell them to bring anything that will hold dirt."

Marya got our largest mixing bowl, Olga a scrubbing pail, and Yelena a wastebasket. We were a strange parade hurrying through the streets. I led them to an excavation to repair a broken sewer line. The dirt from the excavation was sitting in a beautiful pile. When the workmen had seen me take the first sack of dirt, they had laughed. "Help yourselves. It will save us the trouble of carting the dirt away. It's a mystery, but when you dig a hole, there is always more dirt left than fits back in."

Now they watched with amusement as we began to scoop up the dirt.

"Well, comrades, if you have a recipe that turns dirt into food, I wish you would share it."

"That's just what we have," I answered.

When our containers were filled, we hurried back to the balcony. By the time we made our third trip, we had an audience. The little knot of people were too puzzled to make fun of us. After all that had happened in the city, no one could tell what strange thing might be done for what strange reason.

One old man cried out, "Scoop up the whole city. It's good for nothing."

At last we had two feet of dirt on the balcony. Although it was nearly midnight, it was still daylight. We sat around talking of what we would plant and what meals we would make from our harvest. Before Yelena and Olga left us, Yelena asked, "I know it's frivolous, but could I plant just a few flowers?"

"Why not?" I said. "Vegetables for the stomach, flowers for the heart."

The next morning I was up at five. "Where are you going?" Marya asked, half asleep.

"I'm going to take the trolley across town to the soldiers' stables where they keep their horses," I said. "We need a little fertilizer for our vegetable garden."

She sat up. "You can't mean to carry manure on

the streetcar! People will laugh at you."

"Who will know what is in my bag?"

"Everyone. It will smell!"

"In the streetcar there will be plenty of smells. No one will notice."

It was early in the morning, so the streetcars were not so crowded. No one looked twice at my empty bags. The parade ground, when I reached it, was deserted, but you could see that plenty of mounted soldiers had been there. A young cavalry soldier came riding out from one of the stables. I wished the earth would swallow me up. I had wanted to be a soldier like he was, and here I was, gathering manure. The soldier only called, "Well, son, that's the best gold of all. Plenty more where that came from." He laughed and swaggered away. I hoped he would fall off his horse and break his neck.

Back on the streetcar I struck up a conversation with the man next to me about how fine it was to have the streetcars running again. After a few minutes the man looked suspiciously at my bags and, getting up, hurriedly moved away. Soon I had a whole section of the trolley to myself.

When she finally stopped laughing at my story, Marya helped me work the manure into the soil. While I had been gone, she had picked up the seeds that were being given out. We made neat rows, planting lettuce, beans, carrots, tomatoes, turnips, and radishes. The seed packets were stuck on little sticks and looked like small, brightly colored flags. I had never put my hands deep into warm earth. It was a strange feeling, almost as though the earth were alive.

Marya held up a package of morning glory seeds. "For Yelena. They can twine around the balcony railing with the cucumbers and squash and won't take up any space."

When all the seeds were planted, I brought a pail of water from the canal, and after carefully watering our garden, I stared at the dirt, hoping a bit of green might show.

That afternoon Yelena rushed into the apartment.

"Georgi, come quickly! Help me!"

I followed her into the Daskals' apartment, afraid of some disaster, though there had been a look of joy on her face.

She pointed. "There, there on the wall."

A yellow butterfly was fluttering about. The cocoon had opened, making a small miracle.

"Help me to get it out the window," Yelena said, "but don't touch the fine dust on its wings."

Together we were a moving barrier, sending the butterfly closer and closer to the window until it flew out. Yelena burst into tears.

I thought that unreasonable. "You wanted it to fly out the window," I accused.

"Yes, yes, I know, but I liked having it in the room with me. It was so . . . so flimsy, yet it survived the winter. Georgi, it was so encouraging."

Late in June we had our first vegetables from the balcony garden. Marya had urged me to wait a week or so before harvesting them. "The lettuce and radishes will be larger by then."

"But not so tender," I said. Recklessly I picked the lettuce. When a row was empty, I quickly planted another row. Yelena came daily to examine the morning glories. Bits of color showed on the tips of their buds, and then one morning I looked out onto the balcony and there was a great blue trumpet-shaped flower, as blue as the bluest sky. This time it was I who ran excitedly for Yelena.

Olga jumped up in alarm, but I said, "It's only a flower."

We all stood looking out at the single flower that had bloomed with the first rays of the sun.

"The flower is a miracle," Yelena whispered.

It had been a year since war had been declared. I thought that after all we had been through, it was amazing that a single flower could make us so happy.

There were gardens like ours all over the city. The official gardens were in parks, but unofficial gardens were to be found everywhere, in pots on windowsills, along stairways, and on rooftops. Wherever you looked, something green was growing; and almost always, as in our own garden, there was a bright flower or two. With the vegetables, people began to appear a little healthier. Fyodor lost his haunted look. Yelena's eyes were a clear blue again and, though I was too embarrassed to say it to her, the color of the morning glories.

Olga was eating each evening with the other members of the orchestra. "Not bad," she said. "Cabbage soup, and sometimes you can see the cabbage." One day she arrived home hungry and in tears. "Eliasberg is so strict. If we are late for practice, our rations are taken from us. He makes no exceptions. I stopped for just a moment to have a word with a friend I met on the street. We congratulated each other on still being alive. I was five minutes late to rehearsal, and Eliasberg said, 'No excuses' and wouldn't let me eat with the others."

I had just picked some beans from the balcony.

Marya cooked them up for Olga, and she began to tell us how rehearsals were going.

"We have to prop up the bass for Anna," she said. "She doesn't have the strength to hold it herself. And our soldier recruits are on duty into the night, so they fall asleep at rehearsals. I don't know how, but we managed to get through the whole first movement of the symphony."

The war and the shelling and the bombing went on. On July 25, Navy Day, a group of German prisoners was paraded down the prospekt. It was the first we had seen of prisoners of war in Leningrad. They were a sad, bedraggled bunch, some of them younger than I was. People lined the streets to stare at them. A few shouted curses and threw things. Dmitry shook his fist at the prisoners, but most of us stood silently, too angry for words or the shaking of fists.

The scene left a bitter taste in my mouth, so when Marya opened the door for me with a huge smile on her face, I said crossly, "If you believe there is anything to be happy about, you are living in another world."

Marya laughed. "You'll soon change your tune, my boy."

Mama was there, Fyodor holding on to her skirts, Olga and Yelena close by. Mama threw her arms around me. "Georgi, where does that bitterness come from? When I left, I left a cheerful son."

I was instantly ashamed. Whatever I had suffered in the city, Mama had surely seen more terrible things at the front. "Where did you come from?" I asked, dancing her about the room, Fyodor laughing and spinning around after us. "How long are you here for?" It seemed too good to be true.

"They are desperate for nurses. I am here to prepare some women for duty at the front. I'll be here until their training is accomplished. Now you must tell me everything you have been up to."

Though I had written Mama, she wanted to hear all about the trips across Lake Ladoga.

Mama said, "We heard at the front about the bravery of the truck drivers and how they saved the city with their cargos of food supplies. Let me tell you, Georgi, what you did was just as important as any soldier's job. You risked your life every time you got into the truck and set out onto that treacherous ice."

I was embarrassed by Mama's words. I had done only what many others had. Quickly I asked, "Mama, was it very bad at the hospital?"

"Yes, Georgi, I can't pretend it wasn't. Every minute there was another tragedy, and the worst thing of all was that the soldiers were getting younger and younger—they were only boys."

She saw the look on my face. I was thinking that on September sixth I would be sixteen. I thought all the time of the soldiers fighting to save our country. I knew I would find a way to join the army.

"Georgi, promise me you won't go do anything you shouldn't."

Perhaps it was a little dishonest, but I promised,

for I didn't think fighting for my country was something I shouldn't do.

Eager to change the subject, I said, "What do you think of our garden?" The door to the balcony was open, and you could see fat tomatoes ripening and the cucumbers hanging on the vines among the morning glories.

"It's a wonder. One of the hardest things to bear on the front was the ruined land. I think if I could have seen a field of wheat or the blossoms of a potato field, the misery would have been easier to endure. Where there had been farms, there was nothing but burned houses and bombed-out craters, no live thing and no green thing. I'll be content to sit here by the hour and devour the sight of your beautiful garden."

That night we had a celebration for Mama's return. Olga and Yelena and Andrei were all there. We picked our first ripe tomato, and I split it seven ways with much direction from everyone about how to make the slices even. Though the soup was thin, the bread was coarse, and afterward my stomach was still empty, I have never had a better meal.

Olga left early one evening for the dress rehearsal. The concert was the following night, August 9. "Tonight will be the first time we have played the whole piece right through," Olga said. "It takes an hour and a half, and there was not the strength to do it before." Yelena and I sat together, waiting up for Olga, for there was a huge amount of bombing going on, but it was from our side. It sounded as if we wanted to destroy the whole German army in one night. When she came in, Olga was breathless with the night's efforts and climbing the stairs.

"We managed it!" she said, flinging herself down onto a chair. "We got through the whole symphony."

True to her word, the next night Olga had seats for Mama, Yelena, Marya, Andrei, and me. A friend from the Hermitage offered to care for Fyodor. We hurried through the little park with its statue of the poet Pushkin and into Symphony Hall. We were among the

privileged, for though we were early, the hall was filling up and long lines were still forming at the ticket
office. We were all wearing our best clothes, which
were little more than rags. I had on my one good shirt,
so thin you could read a book through it. Yelena wore
the dress I remembered from our picnic at the Summer
Garden.

She laughed when I complemented her. "Georgi,
there is more mending than material! I only hope it
lasts through the concert. Certainly I can't move an
inch."

The hall was impressive with its red velvet and its
tiers of boxes that had once held the aristocrats of St.
Petersburg. I caught Mama looking up at what had
been the royal box, where she had sat with the tsar
and the empress and their children.

Suddenly something startling happened. There
was a brightness all about us. Electric lights had lit up
the stage. It had been months since anyone had seen
an electric light. All around me people gasped with

surprise and pleasure. One by one the musicians walked onto the stage. You could see they were making a great effort to walk briskly and carry themselves well, but every few seconds one or the other would have to slow a bit or shift the weight of an instrument from one hand to another. The musicians were thin and shabby, but on their faces was an expression of great pride, as if they were kings and queens. There were cheers and applause. After they were seated, the conductor, Eliasberg, walked onto the stage amid great applause and bowed to the audience. He raised his baton. The hall was silent. The music began.

Though for weeks I had heard Olga's violin through the walls of our apartment, and though Mama always had on the broadcasts of the philharmonic orchestra, still I knew little about music. I liked popular tunes better, but the Shostakovich symphony pounded you over the head with its power. First came something that sounded like an

evil army marching in the distance and then pounding drums, coming closer and closer. Next there was sad, waiting music followed by music that grew louder and more exciting. The excitement died down, and Olga, her face shining, played a violin solo. Yelena squeezed my arm so hard I nearly yelped. The music grew stronger and stronger and ended in a great victorious crash. We all felt it was the Russians defeating the German army.

When the music ended and Eliasberg put down his baton, and the members of the orchestra put down their instruments, there was complete silence in the hall. We were all in a trance, bewitched, we couldn't move. Someone in the audience stood up and began to clap, someone else followed. Soon everyone was standing, and the hall was shaking with the sound of applause. The audience could not get enough. They kept calling Eliasberg back. A little girl ran up onto the stage with a bouquet of flowers as big as she was— they must have been all the flowers blooming in

Leningrad. We clapped one another on the shoulders, and wiping away our tears, we finally made our way out into the park.

The sound of a shell falling somewhere in the city startled me. "It was amazing," I said. "There was no sound of artillery during the symphony."

Andrei smiled his knowing smile. "That was no accident. All the shelling you heard last night, that was our soldiers giving the Germans everything we had. We wanted to knock them back on their heels so that we would not have to put up with their bombs tonight."

Later we heard that the German army had listened to the symphony on their radios. So much power must have had them shaking in their boots.

Early in September we dug up the first turnips. They were still small, but the days were growing shorter and we were already having frosts. The beans were used up and the tomato vines were turning brown. Blooms on the morning glories were scarce and frazzled. On September sixth Mama harvested the last of the vegetables, a fat squash that she cooked to celebrate my sixteenth birthday.

The next day I joined the Russian army.

AUTHOR'S NOTE

On the night of January 18, 1943, the troops on the Russian front joined forces. After 526 days the blockade of Leningrad was partially broken. January 27, 1944, marked the true end of the blockade. The Siege of Leningrad had lasted 880 days. On May 8, 1945, World War II in Europe came to an end.

GLOSSARY

blini: a pancake filled with fruit or cheese

burzhuika: small stove

gastronom: grocery store

Gostiny Dvor: combination marketplace and flea market

krendeli: little heart-shaped cookies

makivneki: sweet rolls with poppy seeds

nichevo: never mind

ostanovka: halt

piroshki: meat pies

prastitye: pardon me

S Rozhdestvom Khristovom: Merry Christmas

unimaniye: attention

voina: war

BIBLIOGRAPHY

Ginzburg, Lidiya. *Blockade Diary*. Trans. by Alan Myers. London: Harvill Press, 1995.

Likhachev, Dmitry S. *Reflections on the Russian Soul: A Memoir*. New York: Central European University Press, 2000.

Lincoln, W. Bruce. *Sunlight at Midnight: St. Petersburg and the Rise of Modern Russia*. Boulder, Colo.: Basic Books, 2001.

Salisbury, Harrison E. *The 900 Days: The Siege of Leningrad*. New York: Harper & Row, 1969.